April Heads For...

Part Two

By Matthew Le

BunnyLovesBigCarrots@gmail.com

Keith found his eyes voraciously consuming her body. He couldn't stop himself. From her pink nipples to her swollen pussy, the signs of James' mauling were everywhere. Her puffy inner-labia peeked between the engorged outer and Keith knew that a flood of cum lay trapped behind.

Are you making a baby with James at this very moment? he wondered.

He waited for the wave of disgust and nausea he was sure would follow such a terrible thought but none came.

For her part, April was performing a slow, internal collapse. Panic swept through first, then shame and guilt. Keith's gaze as it traveled her body seemed to vivisect her, one guilty part at a time. She wanted to shrink and escape through the carpet fibers. She wanted to evaporate before his burning, incriminating stare and drift away. She took halting steps towards him, trying to read his face, trying to understand what emotions moved him. She hugged herself as she moved closer, trying to hide her nakedness, her face twisted with concern and compassion.

"Oh, Baby, talk to me. What are you feeling? What did you see? Did you see everything? I won't blame you for hating me. I hate myself right now."

Tears welled in her eyes and her lips trembled. Keith saw her eyes dart to the semen running down the inside of the closet door.

Can I even be outraged? He wondered. *Can I even be all that hurt?*

She stopped inches from him, heat rising from her recently fucked body. He smelled sperm and sweat and alcohol.

If I wouldn't have just climaxed, I'd be rock hard right now.

Titanic forces surged in him, pulling in so many directions he was rendered stationary. Anger rose but before he could frame it lust swept in and knocked anger flying. Hurt flared, and self-pity, but hot on their heels came the realization he'd arranged for them to be alone. He'd encouraged her.

I didn't tell her to fuck him but alone together in a hotel room was my idea, not hers. What did I think would happen? What did I want to happen, truly?

He drew a huge breath, filling his lungs all the way to the soles of his feet.

But if I let her off the hook, there'll be no stopping her.

"Baby?" she pleaded.

He tilted his head back and yelled an animal cry of frustration at the ceiling. April flinched and closed her eyes, ready for whatever came at her. Keith saw her prepared to take a hit and his heart broke. His arms shot out and encircled her in a fierce hug. The dam burst. Tears flowed as she wept against his chest. She stood, feeling unworthy and underserving, and accepted his unconditional love. He squeezed tighter.

"April, I would never hit you. Never ever, for any reason."

She leaned into him but said nothing, sobbing, slowly fighting for self-control. He moved his arms up to bear-hug her head, which he kissed.

"Do you hate me?" she whimpered at last.

"No."

"What then?"

"Good question." He forced his mind to focus. *What am I feeling most?*

April waited, tugging at the loose skin on her hand.

"Why?" he asked. "Why did you do it?"

She drew a breath to answer.

"No. Wait," he interrupted. "I probably know most of your reasons *why* already and that's not what I'm after. What I want to know is did you fuck him because you want to be with him and not me? Have I lost you to him?"

Her red eyes grew big. Her jaw dropped open. "No! No way. Not at all. What I did with James has nothing to do with my feelings for you. I just wanted James. Every girl wants James."

"This goes all the way back to high school?"

"Yes. I was selfish and thoughtless. I hope you can forgive me. I hope you can trust me again."

He watched her closely, almost ready to reveal what he knew. "Because James was the guy all the girls wanted. Every girl wants him so he has his choice and he picked you. That made you feel special."

"Exactly."

"But that doesn't explain Ryan."

Something in his voice had changed. She'd always heard a grain of doubt; Keith was never completely sure if she had or not. That element was gone now. She did not know how or why but sometime between this moment and the last time they discussed Ryan, Keith had gained insight. He knew. For a split-second she considered the same game of dodgeball she'd played before but her gut told her that time had passed. Her husband needed truth.

"Did you fuck him?" he asked, but she heard he already knew.

"Yes."

"Bare?"

"Yes."

"He came inside you?"

Her lips started to tremble again. "Yes."

"Why? Why did you do it? Are you unhappy with me? With this marriage?"

April sighed, sure her marriage was dying. *If I tell him the truth, he'll lose all respect for me.* She sighed again, weary.

Keith waited.

She drew a ragged breath.

"Because he was big."

Her answer caught Keith unprepared. He met her eyes, expecting she teased him, but saw only an embarrassed admission of truth.

"What?"

"I know. It's a horrible reason. I wish I had better, believe me."

"Honestly?"

"Yes!"

"You had sex with Ryan because he has a big cock?"

April flinched. "God, that sounds awful. I could blame it on the weed, or the sex games we played on the drive out, or your reaction when I blew David, or a million other factors, but, ultimately, when he took it out, it was big and hard and beautiful and I wanted it."

Keith studied her face. She knew she'd crossed a line but she'd been unable to resist. *April couldn't stop herself because Ryan had a big cock. James does too and that probably swayed her as well. Why does that make me hot?*

"So, again, nothing to do with your feelings about me."

"Nope."

Keith rubbed both hands up and down his face. April timidly met his eyes. She placed a small hand over his heart.

"You're afraid I don't love you," she said. "Lack of love is often a reason people cheat but it's not the only reason. It's not that simple. I've been thinking about this a lot lately. What they teach us about sex and love is wrong. I see the world differently. We're told that if you love someone you could never do that to them, but I do love you. I never stopped loving you. I'm *in* love with you. I just think more like a man on this subject. What I did with them has nothing to do with you and me and everything to do with me and them. In my mind, you and I are rock solid. I know this sounds like I'm trying to sell you on the idea but I'm not. If you said we were finished with these games and no one else ever again, I'd abide by that. I swear."

She took his hands in hers before continuing.

"I won't bore you with my rationalizations; Ryan had a large cock and I wanted sex with it, pure and simple. It helped that he was gorgeous and dashing and I was high as fuck, but I've discovered I have a thing for big cocks. I don't know what it is. I love the way they look. I'm drawn to them. I swear they call to me. I've fucked two and I love them. I'll stop if you demand it but I'm hoping you don't. I'm hoping you can see what I'm saying. Your reaction to my infidelities must give you some insight. I know you love me although you push me at other men."

Keith sat on the couch and looked up at her. April hugged his head against her stomach. Keith closed his eyes.

"Please tell me we're okay," she murmured.

He wanted to say the words but couldn't. Despite all his contributions to her betrayals, he still believed April cheated. She alone pulled the trigger. If he said they were okay, he knew what he was truly agreeing to.

April would be free to do whatever she wants.

His eyes opened.

But didn't I recently tell her that? I told her never do something because she thought it's what I wanted. I told her I wanted her to act on her own ideas. I told her I would not freak out if she did. Now I'm afraid to let her have the very thing I said I wanted her to have. I'm such a chicken-shit.

He looked up at her gorgeous, tear-stained face. He stood and kissed her softly and moved his mouth near her ear.

"We're okay."

He felt her tense body relax a little. He nudged her at the couch and she sat and he knelt and spread her legs. Her slippery labia parted.

"Baby? No, Honey. Wait."

He did not wait. He lowered his mouth to her clitoris and lapped at it. Shivers rocked April.

"Unngh, Christ, Honey, what are you doing?"

He tried not to think about James in there. Keith desperately needed to reclaim his woman and without an erection, this was the only way.

I want to hear her cum. I need it.

He put his tongue to work, pushing every button she had. Slowly, pleasure forced through the maelstrom of other emotions. The relief she felt threatened to make her cry again. Keith set her legs on his shoulders and pulled her round butt to the edge of the couch.

All or nothing, he thought, just before he pushed the length of his tongue inside her. April groaned and put both hands on the back of his head. Her time with James ended too abruptly and she was pleased to discover she carried incredible sexual tension still. Keith's tongue was magic. She felt like a princess with her many suitors all trying to win her heart and she let herself enjoy it for a moment. Memories of James drifted by as Keith worked her pussy like an expert and she made that sound she always made. Keith heard it and doubled his efforts. April gripped the hair on his head.

"Fuck, Baby, that's so good. You do me just right. Make me cum, Lover."

She called him Baby and he remembered she called James that too. His limp penis twitched. He ate her faster, determined to make her cum hard.

"You loved that big cock," he heard himself say.

Tension flashed through her body. When she was silent he wondered if he'd awakened her guilt but then she spoke, cautiously: "I did."

"You looked so sexy, April. My dick was so hard."

She relaxed some. "Was it? You like watching me get fucked, Baby?"

"I love it but I get frightened." He licked all around and then slipped inside again. April moaned.

"Because you see what his cock does to me. You should have been there when Ryan fucked me. Such a stud. He came in me three times, Lover."

Keith felt his heart flip and thump in his throat. *Three times!* He saw April on her back with legs spread wide, on all fours, pussy waving in the air, sitting on top, riding Ryan like a horse. He kept licking as he asked his next question: "How many times did you cum, Baby?"

She ground her dripping pussy against his mouth, inching closer to orgasm.

"Oh, fuck! Every time he did, Honey. I came when he came. Every time he shot me full he drove me over the edge and I came all over his hard cock. Oh, fuuuuuck!"

Keith held her firm ass as she climaxed. Her hips bounced all over as she pulled his mouth tightly to her cunt and screamed wild sounds of pleasure. Keith lapped her juices and did his best to push her higher. She came a long time and he realized she was still turned-on from earlier with James. When she was about to come down he whispered: "Maybe you should fuck James again tomorrow?" and that set off an explosion deep in her womb. Her pussy gushed and she groaned and writhed until her spine popped. He left her drained and limp.

After some time, he helped her to bed and she woke him an hour later to make love. Keith felt his penis slide into the hot slick tunnel of her pussy and knew that was James all around him and he got so aroused he came too fast. Later they woke and did it again but this time she stopped as she rode him and asked if she'd hurt him.

"No. Yes. My head's a mess, Honey. My heart too. This is all so new I don't yet know what to do with all I feel. I'm stumbling forward blindly."

"Me too," she said. "I've never been this girl. I've never had problems like this. I've never had to think about these things and I get so excited that I am this girl now, the girl that the guys want, I get intoxicated by it and don't think things through."

"You think with your dick."

She laughed. "Yeah, I guess I do. Forgive me?"

"I would if I needed to but I've had a hand in everything you've done."

She rocked her hips gently, looking down at her husband. A sly grin curled her mouth. "I'm going to fuck James tomorrow."

He stiffened and knew she felt it inside. Her eyes gleamed.

"No more behind your back, though, Baby. I understand now how that makes you feel left out and threatened."

She put her hands on his chest and brought her elbow together, thrusting her big teardrop tits out.

"From now on, unnggh, I'll fuck them all right in front of you. Agggh, fuck, I'm going to cum again. I don't believe it. I'm so happy I get to be the hot girl, Baby. I never thought I'd be the hot girl. Guys want me now. James Thomas fucked me. Unngh, I love it. I fucked James Thomas."

Keith felt his cum rising. He held her hips to keep her seated and watched her orgasm build. She grabbed her tits hard and pinched her nipples.

"Say his name," Keith said. "Pretend I'm James. Close your eyes. Say his name."

April squeezed her eyes shut and circled her hips around Keith's erection.

"Oh fuuuuuck, James. I love it. I can't believe you're fucking me. Cum in me, Baby. I wanted you so much for so long and then it was you who wanted me. Unnngh! I'm almost there. Fuck me, James. Fuck me like you did last night! Fuck! Fuck!"

April's climax smashed into her.

"Aaaaaaaa! God!"

Her head wobbled and her body shook and Keith knew in her mind she rode James. He felt no jealousy. April was stunning when she orgasmed. She collapsed onto his chest and he rolled her aside. He got behind her and stuffed a pillow under her hips and pushed himself back in, using her limp body to please his dick. After a few minutes, she began lifting her hips to meet him. His last thought before cumming was spraying his semen in the mix with James'.

The rising sun woke them and they fucked again.

"What a night," Keith said after they finished.

April rested in the crook of his arm with her head on his chest. She played with his light chest hair. "What a night," she agreed. "I won't keep anything from you again but that still leaves a lot of things undetermined. I guess we figure stuff out as we go?"

"What stuff?"

"Well, if we could reverse time, would you have let me fuck Ryan and James if I told you that's what I wanted beforehand?"

Keith stared at the carpet. "Yes, I have to admit I would have."

"So it's not even the sex, it's the leaving you in the dark about it."

"Yes."

"You're fine if I fuck someone else, you just do not want to be made a fool."

Keith laughed. "God, that makes me sound so lame."

"Not at all. It's humiliating and not in a good way. Women hate that shit. Being the last to know is the worst. I'll do as you ask but I think part of you likes the torture. Maybe you want it this way because it's so new and scary. I'll bet you a dollar you are soon comfortable with me acting impulsively again."

"I take that bet."

They shook hands.

"I'm still going to fuck with you though. I know where the line is now and I won't cross it, but I'll get my toes right up to it."

Keith was unsure what she meant so he dropped it. She'd told him what he wanted to hear and that was enough. They'd survived a crisis and felt closer than ever. Breakfast was delightful and they went for a long walk afterwards.

Back at the hotel room they started to dress for the park and April spread her outfit on the bed; white shorts, no panties, a baby blue tank top with a dark blue bikini top underneath.

"Exactly what James told you to wear," Keith noted.

"His wish is my command," April teased.

Keith winced. Some aspects of their new life took getting used to. That she dressed to please James titillated Keith but made him queasy too. Keith put on his cargo shorts and a button up short sleeve shirt and his strappy sandals.

They met at Barnett Park so there were baseball diamonds, soccer fields, a gym, and even boating on Lawne Lake. In the center was a small island covered in trees and vegetation. The crowd from the night before had grown five times with the addition of husbands, wives, boyfriends, girlfriends, friends, and children.

April found a gathering of friends she liked and joined them. Introductions were made for Keith again and everyone began talking about work and school and kids and life. Keith kept an eye out for James and when he saw him an hour later, his heart skipped. He discretely nudged April's knee under the table and she casually looked around and Keith was looking right at her when her face softened and then blushed.

James had friends scattered all over so he took some time working his way around to April but once their eyes met, sparks flew. They were careful but Keith saw it and the now familiar tingling in his balls started again.

I don't know why I love it, but I do.

James joined the conversation.

Much later, someone mentioned the ice was running low but the boathouse had more. April volunteered to go and turned to Keith.

"Help me carry it back?"

He smiled at his pretty wife. "James," he said. "You're a big guy. Would you mind? I twisted my knee working out and it's still sore."

"Not at all. Happy to help." He faced April. "Ready?"

She kissed Keith on the lips half a heartbeat too long and cut across the park with James. Keith waited until they were out of sight and then mentioned he forgot his phone in the car and would return. He circled in the opposite direction, looping around to the boat house and spying them through a small open window. The trek took longer than he thought so when he found them in the kitchen, they were already kissing like lovers long separated. James held her face in both hands but her hands were busy, roaming every inch of his strong body. Her right hand found his cock and squeezed his fat dick through his jeans.

"Does your husband suspect?"

"No," April said. "He suspects nothing because he was hiding in the closet and saw everything."

James quickly stepped back. "What?"

Keith recoiled too, unsure how he felt about James knowing. A wave of mild humiliation passed through him. *James gets to fuck her and knows I know. Ouch. What an ego trip for him.*

"Yes," she continued. "He confronted me as soon as you left. He was hurt but not as badly as you'd expect. He said watching me get fucked was hot. He jacked-off while he watched us."

"No shit?"

"No shit. Why do you think he sent you with me for ice?"

James reached for his zipper. Down it went and he pulled his soft cock through the hole. He tangled his fingers in April's hair and tried to force her to her knees. She resisted.

"You think you can just whip it out and I'll suck it?"

"Yes." He forced her down again and this time she went, laughing. April opened her mouth wide and pushed him in. Only half of that thick shaft fit but that was enough to rip a deep moan from James. He looked down at her pretty face.

"I've wanted my cock in your mouth every second since I left last night." He eased in and out and April let him control things. "Fuck, you grew up gorgeous."

April was already wet. James' aggression expressed his desire and April wanted to be wanted. He told her to play with her pussy while she was down there and she replied she already was.

Keith saw that fat tool disappear into his wife's mouth and heat rose in his belly. Like a pink python, the soft cock bent and coiled as April sucked it. Her cheeks dented whenever she sucked hard. She forced as many inches as deep as she could but only took about half. James held her there gazing down into her eyes.

"When can I fuck you again?"

April withdrew his meat and held the slobbery shank straight up. "Whenever you want. Let's hang out with everyone for a while to dispel rumors and then sneak away."

"What about your husband?"

"Good question. Let me talk to him." She stood. "We better get back."

Keith double-timed it around the baseball field back to the bench and was casually talking with a woman named Brenda when James and April reappeared with ice. James opened each bag and dumped them into coolers. April leaned close to Keith.

"He wants to fuck me right now. I sucked his cock for a minute in the kitchen."

"Did you tell him I knew?"

"Yeah, I told him you watched. I hope that's alright. It just seemed the easiest way to make things work."

James came around the table and sat next to Keith and across from April. Keith couldn't help himself and glanced down at James' bulge. The group sat and talked and Keith felt a growing lust.

I'm sure April and James feel the same.

Brenda mentioned she drove a sixty-five Mustang and Keith feigned interest in it.

"I'd love to see it. Are you parked close?"

"Over by the south entrance. Come on, I'll show you." She stood and looked across the table. "I'm going to borrow your husband for a bit," she told April.

Keith and April locked eyes.

"Okay, just bring him back in one piece."

Keith kissed April softly and walked away with Brenda to see the car. April waited a minute and then asked those at the table where the restroom was. A woman April did not know pointed at a small brick building and April rose to leave.

"Don't go by yourself, Sweetie. Take someone with you. Be safe."

"I'll escort you," James offered.

Keith saw them walking across the park and smiled.

The building had men's and women's and James backed into the men's side slowly unzipping his pants. As the brick opening swallowed him, he flopped his dick out like a worm on a hook. April watched, giggling. She still couldn't believe the one and only James Thomas flirted with her. She had his full attention. She scanned the park to determine they were alone and followed James into the men's side. He moved to the far stall and opened the door and waved April in, stepping in after her. He locked the door.

"Be quiet," he said.

She tried to kneel, ready to suck again, but he caught her under the arms and lifted her to the toilet seat. He crouched and pulled her shorts aside.

"Just like I asked," discovering she wore no panties.

"Of course," she said.

He licked her entire pussy with one broad swipe and she covered her mouth with both hands.

James Thomas is giving me head!

She opened her legs wider and he dove in.

Keith arranged this, she told herself. *I'm almost positive this is totally fine.*

James buried his tongue deep inches inside and April bit her knuckles.

Holy fuck!

His long tongue wiggled and writhed and April crossed her legs around his head. He was masterful. Someone entered the restroom and used the first stall and then washed their hands and left and James never stopped licking and sucking. April was driven mad. He focused his attention on her clit while pumping her pussy with a thick finger and April could no longer hold back. She covered her mouth with both hands and clamped her jaw shut and climaxed hard and long.

James gave her no respite. He lifted her to her feet and peeled off her shorts and then made her kneel on the seat, her pussy in his face. He aimed his huge cock from behind and pierced her tight cunt, reaching around to cover her mouth with her shorts. He steadied her with the other hand and began a long and deep in and out rhythm, resting the plump head just within her labia and then sliding inside all the way to his balls. The sensation was wonderfully excruciating for both.

April felt another climax building already. To be turned around like some hot slut and fucked in a public men's room aroused her more than she understood. She felt slutty and bad and loved it. She imagined how they looked together; James fucking April, and her pussy clenched around his wide hard shaft.

James is fucking me, she thought. *James is fucking ME.*

She grew lightheaded and only his strong hand kept her on the seat. His cock sank into her guts on every stroke. She felt filled by him, dominated and owned by him. When he gasped in pleasure she felt a thrill race through her body and her climax begin. He felt it too in the further tightening of her pussy around his meat. He pumped faster, his cum starting to boil up from his big balls. He felt a special added delight because she was married, because he'd met the husband, and because the husband was aware his wife was getting fucked.

"Fucking hot married slut," James moaned.

April moaned too, shoving her tight pussy back at him. He clamped the material around her mouth to smother her cries and squeezed his lips tight. Her spine twisted and he knew she was cumming on his cock and he threw his head back in a silent roar as he fired the first of many searing bolts of sperm far up inside her. The length of her body shook as she gave herself to him. He filled her married pussy with hot semen.

Many minutes passed before they were ready to move. They dressed in silence and James exited first and them whistled an all-clear. April kissed his cheek as she passed and they aimed for the party. She thought she felt his load slosh once or twice on the way back and grinned.

Keith was waiting at the bench, deep in conversation with a bearded man April did not recognize. She sat next to her husband and Keith lightly kissed her ear, showing no outward sign of concern. She acted utterly nonchalant and chatted with the others. Only when she moved to lean closer to Keith and her wrist contacted the straining erection under his cargo shorts, did she realize he knew. She settled her back against his chest and exhaled slowly.

After a while James got a call on his cell and wandered away from the group. April asked if Keith wanted to walk around the lake and Keith said that sounded like a great idea. They grabbed fresh bottles of water and set off.

As soon as they were out of ear-shot Keith spoke: "Did you fuck him?"

"Yes! Oh, Baby, it was fantastic. From behind his cock feels even bigger. I came so hard. I feel so deliciously slutty."

"Did he cum?"

"Yes, deep inside me. I swear I feel him splashing around. Those big balls make a lot of sperm."

Keith groaned.

"You okay, Honey?"

"Yeah," he said, breathless. "This is so intense."

"I love it. I bet you're dying to fuck me, or maybe eat me." She giggled.

He steered them towards the shore. She held his hand as they walked.

"What's next?" he wondered.

"I'd love to fuck him again. I'm hoping after the picnic he comes back to our hotel room with us. You can hide in the closet if you want but since he knows about you, maybe you should just pull up a chair to the side of the bed?"

"Not join in?"

"Two men at once? Wow. Honestly, I never thought of that. That seems a bit much. If it's okay with you I'd like a rain-check. I know some girls do that but I've only been this girl for such a short time. I'm not ready to be that girl. Besides, there's something special about James Thomas in my bed. I'm not ready for two men at the same time, Honey. That sounds too slutty. I hope that doesn't hurt your feelings."

"It does, a little, but the hurt feels good in a strange way. Let's finish our walk and go hang out with everyone and when the party winds down, bring him home."

April grabbed Keith and kissed his mouth. "You're an amazing man!"

Hours later Brenda fell in the lake and had to be pulled out and Mike backed into a dumpster. Everyone agreed they'd all had enough beer and wine-coolers and finished their hotdogs and hamburgers and said their goodbyes. April never got a chance to invite James back to the hotel so she asked Keith to do it.

"You want me to summon a man back to the hotel room to fuck my wife?"

"Um, yeah. Is that bad?"

Keith shook his head in disbelief.

"Everyone is watching us now. I've talked to him too many times today. They're suspicious. If you talk to him, it's just a couple of guys shooting the breeze."

Keith helped clean up the park, slowly working his way closer to James. When they had a moment alone, he spoke: "April wants you to come to our hotel."

"I don't do gay stuff. No offense."

"None taken. I don't either."

"Threesome?"

"No, she wants you. She wants me to watch. I want to watch too. We both want me to watch."

James smiled. "You guys have no experience at this, do you?"

"None. It's the craziest thing we've ever done and we're making it up as we go."

He put an arm around Keith's shoulders and squeezed. "No worries. I'll be there at seven."

They shook hands and Keith carried trash to the dumpster. Later, he returned to April and told her the time. Her eyes lit up and Keith flinched at how happy the idea of more sex with James made her. They left the park and grabbed dinner and got back to the hotel room early.

Keith showered away the day and then April disappeared into the bathroom reappearing twenty minutes before James was due. She wore a pale blue teddy Keith had never seen before. The top was billowy with long sleeves and utterly see-through. A white bow tied between her breasts. The panties were nothing but a thin triangle of lace. Keith saw the split of her labia clearly.

She was a Christmas present wrapped for James. Angst returned, chilling his blood and souring his stomach. April watched his eyes on her and smiled softly.

"You believe he'll love it," she murmured.

"I know he will."

"That's all I want."

She took his hand and led him to the bedroom and showed him where to move the leather chair; in the corner, deep in shadow. She dimmed lights and turned back the covers. She faced her husband. "Honey, this is so exciting."

He nodded agreement, not trusting his voice to sound steady.

"Undress," she said. "And sit. I want you to know I know what this will do to you, watching me with him. I want you to promise you won't masturbate, or if you must touch yourself, at least don't cum. I'll need you hard after he leaves. Promise?"

"Have you done this kind of thing before, bedroom cop?" he joked. "You're so composed."

"It's all an act, Baby. I'm as nervous as you. Promise?" She folded her arms under her tits.

"Promise." Keith began to strip. He was down to his boxers when there was a knock at the door.

"Finish," she said. "I'll greet him and bring him back. Sit and wait for me, okay?"

He tried to swallow, failed, gave her a quick nod.

April left. He heard the door open and James make a long, low, approving sound. Keith pushed his boxers down and dropped them on the pile of clothing. He sat. Muffled voices drifted down the hall and then tense silence. He knew at that moment James kissed his wife. He tried to prepare himself for what was to come but had no idea where to begin. On its own, his penis began to rise. He looked down at it.

"No conflict whatsoever for you, is there?" he murmured. His rose until fully hard and bounced slightly with each heartbcat. "Fuck."

Footsteps came down the hall and April entered the bedroom, leading James. She'd undressed him in the living room and Keith felt a punch to the gut. The man's enormous cock stuck straight out, half-hard and already so much bigger than his own, with a gleam of saliva all over the head and a few inches behind. She'd dropped to her knees and sucked him the moment he stepped inside.

She backed James towards the bed and once he was seated began a slow strip tease. She did not look at her husband.

She had no talent or experience performing but with her beauty and body, neither man cared. She moved slowly and sensuously, revealing herself a tiny bit at a time. Both men had seen her nude multiple times, yet they sat mesmerized.

Keith's penis pulsed. She still hadn't looked at him and the effect it had was intense. By ignoring him the message she sent was everything she did was purely for James. For reasons Keith did not understand, that aroused him wildly. April had two penises rising to her but her preference was obvious. James was a strong man, burly and thick, just like his cock, and April could not pull her eyes away.

Keith began slow and deliberate masturbation.

God, I love how much she wants him. He made a face. *No, not him; I love how much she wants sex with him. I love how much she loves his big cock.*

April continued her display, each tiny step taking her closer to James. Soon she moved between his knees, twisting and turning, but the man kept his hands on his lap. Keith admired his willpower. At last April turned to face her new lover and pinched the ends of the bowtie between her tits. She gently pulled in opposite directions and her diaphanous top drifted apart, freeing her naked breasts. James looked ready to attack but sat calmly. He was fully erect now, a hefty spear pointed at the ceiling, a clear dollop of pre-cum sitting like a jewel atop the slit. Keith stared at the man's cock and wished his own looked the same.

April was ready. She shimmed her shoulders and the top fell to the floor and then she tugged the tie at her hips and the lace triangles fell too. Keith sensed she had intended to tease James further but her own spell backfired on her; she was as aroused as the men. She lifted a knee over her lover's thigh and then did the same on the other side. Keith held his breath.

April raised her hips and reached under and Keith saw that glittering crown jewel of milky fluid had grown into a large bead the size of a pea. April held the trunk of the shaft with one hand and with the other spread her pussy lips wide. She lowered her hips. Keith witnessed that dewdrop move deep inside his wife before her snug labia closed behind the head, enveloping James in white hot pleasure, her smooth lips traveling slowly down the shaft as she used her body weight to sink onto his cock.

Keith groaned involuntarily.

April did not hear her husband's groan because of her own. James' cock was a cannon penetrating her body, shoving flesh aside as he forced her to take the shape of him. Her head fell back and she held on at his shoulders, forcing her hips down to capture him. Moments later when her head came up, Keith knew she'd taken every inch. Her body radiated stuffed satisfaction. A smile curled the corner of her mouth and she cupped a breast and offered the nipple to James' mouth. He licked first and then softly sucked it in.

James let April fuck him. Keith watched his wife savor every inch of the man, from his bulging chest to his steely cock. She never looked at her husband and Keith had never been harder.

"You're so beautiful," James said. "I want to put a baby in you."

"Okay," April replied.

Keith's jaw dropped open and his mind lit up like a Christmas tree. April's casual reply stunned him.

Such talk was way beyond acceptable. True, they were way out of bounds now, bending rules to the breaking point, but that subject was taboo. He felt rattled. A bomb had exploded inside his head. The room tilted a little and he felt himself disconnect from the scene before him.

When he came back he felt warm liquid flowing over his testicle. His upright penis had leaked several globs of semen without being touched, yet remained solid and throbbing. April groaned with excitement. He looked up to find his wife fucking James with a sensuous and womanly rolling of her hips. James was fully embedded and April ground her clit against his pubic bone, lost in the pulsation of his deeply buried cock. Keith had never seen her fuck this way.

At last, James lifted his hands to touch her. He placed them on her undulating hips and each time she reached a low point, he pressed down, pushing the last remaining inch of his cock into her, reaching far up inside.

Whatever his long shaft touched had a dramatic effect on April. The first-time James bumped the spot her eyes flew wide open. After that her brow furrowed deeply and she emitted a low moaning sound from the back of her throat. Keith saw her quickly anticipate the most penetrating moment and begin assisting James to get deeper.

"Ooooooooh….Aaahhh…mmmmmm, Oooooh."

She leaned forward and wrapped both arms around the man's head. They kissed slow and deep and Keith heard that familiar pre-orgasm moan. James moaned too. Their rocking hips took on more sped and soon April hugged James tightly. Her toes curled and she exhaled a long groan into his neck.

"Give it to me, Baby," James urged. "You love me in there. Cum for me."

April's hips moved mere inches back and forth but Keith knew she was cumming hard. James' cock was a spike driven into her guts, and anchor fastening her to her lover. She felt filled, stuffed.

When the tension in her body began to ebb, James hooked her behind her knees and lifted her as he stood, spinning to face the bed and placing her on her back. He bent her legs up over her tits and slowly long-stroke his slab of beef in and out. Keith thought she looked obscene; ass and pussy spread and lewd. James held her shoulders and fucked her faster until shaking his head slowly as his hips came forward.

"Almost there," murmured. "Close. Here it comes, April."

Her eyes were closed, savoring the huge cock that moved within her.

"Yeah, oh, fuck, yeah. Ooooooh, yeahhhhhhh!"

James pushed his cock deep and held it there as his testicles blast buckets of cum. Keith felt more semen dribbled down his rampant penis and shook his head sadly. He realized many of his truest desires were mysteries to him. He reached for his penis and began stroking. James was filling his wife with white-hot sperm and it was one of the most erotic things Keith had ever seen. He simply could not hold back. He had no defenses against this kind of attack. He wanted to see April fucked. He loved watching April fucked. He *wanted* James to flood her pussy.

Seconds later he groaned and shot a spout of semen. He jacked faster, emptying his nuts as James emptied his. Keith was too busy watching that big cock pump so he missed it completely, but April recognized Keith's groan and turned her head to watch, a sly smile curling her lips. She turned her attention back to James and pulled his mouth down to hers.

Keith and April lay holding hands in the blazing Florida sun the next day, sweating out all the beer and wine from the party.

James had stayed until four in the morning. He fucked April three more times, saturating her with seed, and Keith masturbated to climax each time James did.

The lovers exchanged numbers and James promised to come visit Las Vegas and April walked him to the door and sweetly kissed him good-bye. She watched through the drapes until he got in his car and drove away and then she ran down the hall to the bedroom, laughing like a crazy woman. Keith had moved to sit on the end of the bed and she plopped down on his lap naked and kissed him like a happy puppy.

"That was the hottest thing ever!" she yelled. "Oh my fucking God!"

With too much energy to contain she stood on the bed and jumped up and down, swinging her arms wildly. "I can't believe I just did that! Holy shit!"

She dropped to her knees behind her husband and hugged him fiercely, kissing his neck and the back of his head. She looked over his shoulder at his deflated penis. "You broke your promise," she teased.

He showed her his palms. "I couldn't resist."

"Too fucking hot, right? I don't blame you. I suspected you wouldn't be able to hold back. I'm learning what my man likes."

"What do I like?"

She flopped onto her back. "A hot and slutty wife. A sex-crazed wife."

"It's true."

"Want to kiss my pussy?" she teased. "You love eating me after I fuck someone."

Keith imagined the ocean of cum she contained. "No, not this time. I have a limit."

"You sure?"

"Yes. I do want to see it though."

"See it? Like just look at her?"

"Yes." He reached for his cell phone. April spread her legs. She grabbed each hamstring and pulled, opening herself to his gaze. He crawled forward and lifted his phone, snapping pictures. April used her fingers to spread her pussy open. After Keith took a few more April asked to see them. Keith lay on his back next to her and scrolled through the snapshots. Her pussy was a mess of juice and sperm, with long strands connecting her butt cheeks. Her outer labia were bright red and her inner swollen purple.

"That's a well-fucked pussy," she joked.

"That's a beautiful pussy," he stated.

"Really? I'll never understand the male aesthetic, but I guess I don't need to. You guys like looking and I like being looked at. That's good enough for me."

She snuggled under his arm and he curled it across her chest, protecting her.

"Too bad you can't get hard."

"You want more cock?"

"I want yours. I guess this is hot and sexy though; I'm filled with James and my man can't do anything about it. That's twisted but hot. Very taboo."

"It's maddening but excites me. What was it like? Being with him?"

"He's so big. Way bigger than you."

Keith scoffed. "No shit. Better?"

April gave her husband a coy smile. "If we leave love out of the picture, bigger is better. I couldn't hide from it. I felt him deep inside me every single moment. There was no escape. His size placed him everywhere all at once. Sensations came at me from every nerve."

"Sounds intense."

"Not the word for it but I don't know which word is. Overwhelming? Overpowering? Divine? I don't know. Addicting, for sure."

Keith lovingly caressed her breast. "I love seeing you like that."

"Then I'm a lucky woman."

They stared at the ceiling.

"Let's go to Playalinda after dawn," she said. "The sun will feel so good on our naked bodies."

"Good idea."

Now, hours later, Keith handed April a bottle of water from the small cooler. Something had been nagging him and he decided to bring it up.

"Last night James said he wanted to put a baby in you."

"Was that fucking hot or what?"

"It was. I leaked cum when I heard it. I was excited but also disturbed. That was hard to hear and seemed to cross a line with me."

April rolled on her side to face him. "Too far?"

"In a way. I mean, you're fucking him, right? Without protection. That outcome is automatically a possibility, even with birth control. But hearing the words made it all so real, and your reaction floored me. You said okay without hesitation."

"I was into it."

"Your desire sounded genuine. Is that how you feel? Do you want a baby with James?"

"In the spirit of things, I did at that moment, but no, of course not. A real baby is different from a fantasy baby. I dream of being a princess but don't want to in fact be a princess. I do want a baby with you though. If that kind of talk with other men is off limits I won't do it."

"It's not, but it gets close. I don't want to shut you down on anything, but I guess this is how we feel our way forward; we try something and then talk about it afterwards. We'll find the edges and discover what's too far. You want to have a baby with me?"

"Okay, and yes, I do. It's getting close to that time. Our careers are running smoothly, we've never been more in love or felt more intimate, my health is at an all-time high; I'm not saying today but soon, I think."

He hugged her and she wiggled into it. "Baby talk after a night like last night."

"Crazy life," she chuckled, rolling onto her back again.

"Crazy life."

The day was lazy. They dozed, swam, ate, dozed again. They talked and kissed and watched all the people stroll by. April had to smile at the volume of men that made a pass. She knew an aerial shot would show her in the eye of a penis tornado. They all acted so casual but she was on to them. She soaked up the attention, hungry for more.

Despite her utter sexual satisfaction from the night before, by midday she was feeling horny again. There were naked men and women in every direction and some of the men had nice bodies. The clear majority were average or smaller, but a few were nicely hung. Keith caught her looking but said nothing.

A black athlete took a spot nearby and April looked at him often. Keith reasoned he was a swimmer because his smooth body was hairless except for eyebrows. He was tall and lean with astonishing definition and a sleek black cock that hung longer soft than Keith's erection hard. High cheek bones and green eyes, combined with his coal dark skin, gave him an exotic look.

April smiled.

"Why are you smiling?"

"That is a beautiful, beautiful man."

Keith looked again. The man had a beach chair that supported his back and allowed him to sit up. A can of Corona beer sat in a holder and the man sipped from it while reading.

Keith could not see the title of the book but the tome was thick. He turned to April.

"Beautiful men make you smile?"

She laughed once, like a cough. "No, knowing I could fuck him if I want makes me smile. Assuming he's not gay or married and would be interested in me, knowing I can have him if I want makes me smile. You think we're just sitting on the beach enjoying some sun but I'm sitting in a circle of possible lovers that extends as far as I can see. It's pure cocaine. I'm a little wet all the time."

She turned on her side and looked at Keith. "Baby, I think about sex twenty-four seven now. It's crazy. Every man I see, I see with new eyes." She rolled onto her stomach and covered her head with her T-shirt. "It's all your fault," she joked.

Keith looked around the beach, trying to see the world through April's eyes. He arrived at Black Athlete and studied the man. Flawless ebony skin drawn tightly over wiry muscles glistened in the bright sunlight. The man had his knees up while he read and Keith saw the hairless ball sack resting on the towel, the long dark black penis draped over the top and extending a few inches down the cloth as well.

"He's very black," Keith murmured.

April giggled. "Are you saying that because his penis is so big?"

Keith laughed. "No, it's his skin. He'd not brown or dark brown; he's black."

"He's striking and interesting. I wonder his ethnicity." April rolled onto her back again and covered her face with her shirt. Keith noticed the man eyeing April on the sly. As always, Keith's inclination was to make an excuse and leave April alone to see what she'd do. He considered a swim but stopped himself.

The man looked at April often so the next time he glanced over, Keith smiled. The man smiled back and Keith waved. He called the short distance across the sand.

"Come join us."

"What are you doing?" April said without moving her shirt.

"Making new friends. It was either this or leave you alone and go swim and hope he introduced himself to you. Here he comes."

Keith stood and extended a hand, his eyes momentarily drawn to the man's heavy black cock swinging and bouncing with each step. April watched it too.

"Hi, I'm Keith. This is my wife, April."

The man shook his hand. "Cameron. Nice to meet you."

April sat up and offered her hand. Cameron shook it gently. April's face was less than two feet from his large dark cock. He seemed not to notice.

"Join us," Keith said, gesturing towards the blanket. "We're just soaking up the heat and drinking. Can I get you a Heineken?"

"No, I'm good, thank you. Where you guys from? Local?"

Keith invited him to sit and explained about the reunion and the drive out. Cameron was from San Diego but now swam for Florida State University.

"Do you know Ryan Hanson?" April quickly asked. "He plays football. Tightend."

"No, but it's a huge campus. Friend of yours?"

April nodded. "We're quite close."

Keith rolled his eyes.

The three sat and talked and the conversation roamed. They discussed everything. April admired Cameron and Cameron admired April and Keith enjoyed the play between the two. After about an hour Cam excused himself to return to his book.

"I'm so sorry. I must have it finished by the weekend."

Keith apologized for taking him away from his studies. Cam returned to his towel and chair and picked up his book.

"That was nice," April quipped.

"You two seemed highly interested in each other."

"Maybe you should go take that swim now?"

"You're a comedian."

Later April said: "I guess we should talk about the trip home, points of interest, cities, things like that."

"Or here's an idea; we push on to Miami, enjoy some nightlife, turn the car in and fly two and a half hours to Houston and drive home from there."

"Or fly five hours to Phoenix and then only need an hour to drive home."

Keith checked his phone and saw she was right. "That sounds pretty good."

"It would allow us to stay in Orlando a few more days, if we wanted."

"True."

They looked at each other.

"Are you thinking about James?" Keith asked.

April shrugged.

"Cameron?"

She shrugged again. "Maybe. Or someone else. Or no one else. Or just hang out with my husband on a liberating nude beach. Or we could go on to Miami."

"Let's go grab dinner and let this idea percolate."

"Okay."

They stayed another hour at the beach and then began to pack. Cameron came over and offered his cell in case they drove back through and Keith told April to give the man hers. She did.

They ate dinner back at the hotel and fell asleep early, drained from the sun.

In the end, they spent two more days and then put Orlando behind them, driving on to Miami. April decided she'd spent enough time visiting old friends and stomping around her home town. The call of the unknown was strong.

"Miami will be far more adventurous than Orlando, so why wait?"

"I'm flexible either way. This vacation rocks," Keith said.

"I hear they have a nude beach, too."

"How'd your Spanish?"

"Decent. How's yours?"

"Non-existent, I'm sorry to say."

"You're from San Diego."

"Sad, isn't it?"

The morning they left Orlando they angled for the coast as the drive down to Miami promised to be spectacular. They hit Freeway Ninety-Five just outside Cocoa West and stayed inland down to West Palm Beach, and then the road moved closer to the coast. The hoped-for views never materialized as the freeway was bordered on both sides by high walls and the terrain was so flat they never rose above it. Mile after mile they saw only concrete and other cars.

"Win some, lose some," April said wryly.

Hours later they slowed as they approached Miami.

"This is exciting," April said. "I came here when I was six and never returned. From what I've read the city has exploded with people and energy. Can we stay on the water? Like cut across Biscayne Bay and get someplace on the Atlantic?"

"Sure."

"Oh! Let's try the Fontainebleau. Pricey but fabulous. In high school, we joked that was where the famous people stayed. I can't believe this time it will be me."

April fished her phone from her purse and started making calls. After a while she covered the microphone and asked Keith; "A room for three-hundred, a suite, five-fifty."

"Suite."

"Sweet!"

She spoke to the clerk a few minutes more and hung up. "I took the suite for two nights with an option to move to a lower room after that. She gave me a good deal. What do you want to do first?"

Keith gave her a wicked look.

"Oh, really? Ready to reclaim what's yours?"

"I am."

Two days later, in what had by now become a shared ritual, April stepped from the bathroom, ready to go, and Keith gawked at his stunning wife.

Her long brown hair was set with heavy waves and her make-up worn much darker than usual. Her dress was a purchase from the five-star shop in the lobby and consisted of sparkling and shimmering silver sequins microscopically connected and tantalizingly see-through all the way around. The garment hung from her shoulders like a lampshade, held by two ultrathin and long straps. In back the dress plunged to the dimples above her butt, in front the fabric seemed to cling to each nipple and nothing else, the straps little more than guide-wires. Her full breasts curved out to each side with cleavage and smooth, tan skin exposed almost to her navel. She wore sheer silver panties and high-heel shoes and nothing else. She held a small glittering silver clutch.

Keith had explored city nightlife as soon as they checked into their suite and found that the hottest club in Miami was coincidentally located on the roof of their hotel.

Tartarus was the reincarnation of the infamous Hellfire Clubs of seventeenth century England and decadence ruled the night. Lavishly appointed, the wait list was long and exclusive but guests of any suite had a spot reserved for them should they choose to use it. He showed April the pictures and she was intrigued. April further researched the place online and announced she had to have a new outfit. Even her sexiest dress was too conservative.

"The reviews on Google say it's better than any Vegas club," April read.

"I find that hard to believe."

Keith looked over her shoulder at the pictures. The women were stunning and barely covered at all but the men wore typical dress shirts and sports coats.

That was two days ago. Since then they'd made love, napped, explored the city on foot, eaten, and, in April's case anyway, shopped.

At this moment, however, he stood flabbergasted, gaping at April. Always beautiful, she had added an intense aura of sexy and Keith could not tear his eyes away. Her use of make-up gave her a darker and more sinister aspect. She looked like a bad girl, which carried a heightened impact because she'd never done it. She turned slightly, showing off, and Keith gulped like a cartoon character.

April giggled. "You are good for a girl's ego."

He thought about warning her to be careful in that dress but decided against it.

Fuck it, he thought. *We're three-thousand miles from home. Who the fuck cares if an adult sees a gorgeous tit? All the women will be dressed like this. They won't look as good, but they'll be dressed like this.*

Keith found his voice: "April, my God, you look beautiful. No, that's not enough. You look spectacular. Really, truly, sexy. Gorgeous."

He offered her his arm and they headed for the elevator, one flight up.

The photographs online were a pale representation of that club in full bloom. As hotel guests, they were shown to the VIP line and entered after a short wait. Inside was the most ostentatious waste of money either of them had ever seen. Not waste in that the club was poorly designed or decorated, but that the ornamentation was so extravagant no human eye could ever take it all in. Half-inside, with domed glass ceiling and virtually naked trapeze artists of both sexes filling the air, and half-outside, with a separate DJ, plush furniture and glass swimming pool under the starry, hot and humid, Miami sky, the place dazzled in every direction.

The club had a dress-code but no woman followed it. Keith tried not to stare but there were simply too many breath-taking ladies. Scantily attired, tight skin of every shade danced everywhere he looked.

April fared only a little better. She rarely found a woman sexually attractive but here that went out the window. Black, Latina, Caribbean, Persian, Arabic, Anglo; everywhere she looked feminine power electrified her. Tits and ass and legs and backs and hair and arms and faces; April was dizzy from skin. Best of all, she now felt like she belonged with those women. She was one of them. As many men turned to stare at her as any other girl in the club and if she was honest with herself, often more.

The men stunned too; dressed more to show financial success and independence, the males were still a smorgasbord of handsome and sexy. April had a hard time trying not to stare and soon gave up, deciding staring was exactly what the night called for. Why put so much effort into turning heads and gaining attention if not to see and be seen?

April steered Keith outside. Booths circled half the pool and they found one open and moved in. A waitress wearing lingerie took their drink order and disappeared into the crowd. A DJ played on a raised dais with the words, "Fais Ce Que Tu Voudras" in glowing red neon above. In front of his podium hot bodies in skimpy outfits writhed. Panties flashed as often as nipples and Keith quickly singled out the women wearing nothing under their clothing at all.

"This place is hot," he breathed, pointing at the words over the DJ. "What's that mean?"

April struggled to remember her high school French. "Something about doing whatever you want."

Their drinks arrived and both sat for a while absorbing the sexy wall of flesh before them. The crowd grew larger and denser. Keith and April sat close to each other and watched humanity swirl by. The music was so loud they vibrated along with their table and seat. Tiny waves sloshed their drinks and rattled the ice. When the waitress came around again Keith ordered three rounds. She raised an eyebrow at him but he lied, explaining friends were coming to join them.

Half an hour later they felt giddy. The alcohol relaxed them and they'd started dancing and having a blast. April starting making out with Keith and the nearby crowd shouted approval so he cupped her breast and they roared. She smacked his hand.

Back at their booth they gulped their drinks and let the sweat dry.

A tall Latina leaned over and, raising her voice over the music, asked if it was just the two of them and when April said yes she pointed to another woman close by.

"My friend turned her ankle. Can she sit with you? We got here late and all the seats are taken."

"Of course," April yelled, sliding around and making room. "How many are in your group?"

"Five. My friend and myself and three men we know from work. They're fun guys. Harmless."

April looked the length of the booth. "There's room for six here so come on in. I dance all night and rarely sit so we can share. It will be tight but so what?"

"You are so nice! Thank you!" She leaned over and gave April a soft peck on the lips and turned to guide her friend to the bench.

Keith could not hear the exchange but just followed April's lead. He pulled April close. "We have new friends?"

"Yes." She quickly explained.

Keith had no complaints. The two women were gorgeous in tight white miniskirts and long dark hair. The guys were friendly. The tall Latina introduced them all.

"I am Victoria but call me Vic. This is Maria. That's Ernie, Rudy, and Michael. Do not call him Mike or Mikey." Their group laughed at the warning so April and Keith smiled. Rudy and Ernie were shorter than Keith but stocky. Michael was an inch or two taller and lean. All three men were dusky skinned, although Rudy and Ernie were darker than Michael. All three had shaggy black hair.

Vic assigned seating, positioning each of them based on how often they expected to head for the dance floor. Maria sat in the middle since her time dancing was over. Keith sat on her right and then Rudy and Ernie. On Maria's left it went Michael and then Vic and April.

Conversation flowed smoothly. Everyone talked at once and the pairings shifted constantly, although no one could speak across the table. The music was simply too loud. Soon April left to go dance and Vic joined her. Keith tried to keep an eye on both. He found himself talking to Maria as Ernie and Rudy were best friends and engrossed in a debate about racecars.

Now that he got a better look at the woman he was pleased he got seated next to her. Her short white skirt rode high and he glimpsed occasional flashes of sparkling panties. Once she pushed her hair behind her shoulders he saw she wore a gauzy see-through top and bra. Small dark nipples stared at him. He looked often, afraid he'd get caught, until he realized she knew what he did and that's why she pushed her hair out of the way.

"You were very kind to let me sit," she yelled.

"No problem."

"And to open your table to my friends. Thank you."

They made small talk and Keith felt a growing crush. He watched April dance less and less until Maria was his sole focus.

April and Victoria danced with each other and then with any who wanted to join. Together they drew the attention of everyone that saw them. April felt intoxicated and sexy and beautiful. Victoria flirted with but never touched her.

After many songs Vic said she needed a bathroom break. April glanced at the booth to let Keith know but saw he was smitten by Maria. Jealousy flashed through her but she chastised herself.

Let him have his fun. You've certainly had yours.

Dizzy from drinking, she took Victoria's hand and wove their way through the throng. The line at the ladies' room was absurd but at last their turn arrived and they could talk in the relative quiet of a shared stall.

"You're an excellent dancer," Vic said.

"Thank you, but so are you."

"You have every man in the club hard in their pants. You don't know how sexy you are."

"Don't make me blush, Vic. I'm just having fun. I have a nice buzz going and I really feel it when I move."

Vic gave her a sly look. "You have a nice buzz but maybe you want to have a better buzz?"

"Sure. Of course. You have weed?"

"Better," Victoria said, opening her clutch. She withdrew a small plastic bag and held April's hand palm up. She dumped a blue pill onto it.

"That's it?"

"Yup. That pill takes whatever you are feeling already and amplifies it about a million times. What are you feeling?"

"Drunk. Horny. Not in that order; horny then drunk."

Victoria laughed. They left the stall and April washed the pill down with water from the sink. The bathroom was packed shoulder to shoulder with hot and sweaty girls. They moved to a corner under an air vent, not ready to go outside yet.

"You need to take your man back to your room," Vic teased. "Make him take care of that horny for you."

April felt naughty. She trusted Victoria and wanted to impress her. She wanted Victoria to know how bad she could be. "Maybe. Or maybe take *a* man back to our room."

Vic grinned. "You cheat on your husband?"

"No, he knows all about it. He likes it. I love big cock and he loves when I behave like a slut."

Victoria laughed loud. "That's awesome. I never would have guessed that about you guys. If you love big cock, Michael's your man. That guy has a horse-dick."

"You've fucked him?"

"Oh yes. All the single girls at work have fucked him. Maria's fucked him too. He's shy and quiet until you get him in bed. That man was built for sex. God put him on this Earth to satisfy women."

"Don't tell my husband about the pill. Let's see if he notices I'm high. He seemed taken with Maria. He can look but not touch."

"That's not fair."

"No, it isn't. Pretty hot, huh? I get to but he doesn't? He likes it. Not a ton of it but when I tease him he gets so hard. I must be really drunk. I'm telling you everything."

Victoria put her arms around April and rested their foreheads together. "April, Honey, you can tell me anything. Everyone does. I can keep a motherfucking secret."

Impulsively, April kissed Victoria's mouth. Victoria returned the kiss instantly.

"Do you like girls, too, April?"

"Not really," April said. "You're super sweet and gorgeous. I love cock. I love big hard cock and fat balls and muscles."

Victoria chuckled and gave April a hug. "Let's go back to our friends. I took a pill too and they should hit soon. Let's dance."

"Okay." April pulled Victoria close and kissed her passionately. The girls left the bathroom and returned to the dance floor. Vic danced a few songs and then had to sit but April felt her nerves growing ever more sensitive and wanted to move.

Back at the booth Keith went to join his wife. Michael and Rudy and Ernie were already dancing so Vic slid in next to Maria.

"Nice people," Maria said.

Vic agreed and then shared what she'd learned.

"This will be fun. April's going to go after Michael. You know that, right, Vic?"

"Oh, I'm counting on it. You never know about people. These two seem so sweet, almost innocent."

Maria laughed. "Got that wrong, didn't we? Do we tell Michael?"

"Hell no. This is better than theater."

They raised their martini's in a toast.

"I'm starting to feel the E so I know April is too."

Maria slipped a hand under the table searching discretely for Victoria's pussy. Vic gasped when she found it.

"You're wet."

"This is sexy. I'd love to see Michael fuck April. She's so pretty. Keith will have serious doubts."

Maria chuckled and slipped a gleaming finger into her mouth. "I'll use my ankle as an excuse to get us all invited to their suite. From there, who knows?"

Keith saw April dancing alone when he approached her. She saw her husband and raised her arms and smiled broadly.

"My sweet Baby!" she cried.

She held his face with both hands and kissed his mouth. They danced and April moved closer until her body rubbed against his. Keith felt her big tits everywhere. He laughed and hugged her from behind and spun her around. Her dress slid off her tits, exposing them briefly, and the surrounding crowd cheered again. April covered up but laughed wildly.

After a few songs Keith was sweaty and, spotting Ernie and Rudy in the crowd, pulled them over to dance with his wife. They looked surprised for an instant but then eagerly complied. Keith returned to the booth.

The night wore on just like that. April touched everyone she could, dancing lasciviously with anyone who'd have her, which was almost everyone, male and female. Keith noticed her nipples had been rock-hard for hours and her eyes big. Everyone took turns dancing with everyone until dehydration, fatigue, and a threatening sunrise gave way to thoughts of calling it a night.

"I hate to ask this," Maria said to April, "but can I crash at your place? I'll be out in the morning as soon as I can and won't make a sound. I can't walk on my foot yet."

"Honey! Don't worry about a thing! You can all stay with us. You're all too drunk to drive anyway. Come sleep it off."

Keith nodded agreement.

They tipped the waitress heavily, gathered their things, and made their way to the elevator, Keith and Michael helping Maria to walk. Victoria took the room key from April and opened the door and the group exclaimed delight when the saw the room and the view of the moon over the dark Atlantic. Keith had left the air conditioner off and the sliding glass door open so fresh sea-air filled the space.

They got Maria situated on the couch and the rest grabbed seats next to her or chairs around the room. Keith offered drinks and started mixing. Victoria sked if she could shower the sweat off and April said she'd show her the master bath. They left. Rudy clicked on the wide screen and found a soccer game and Ernie pulled his chair around to watch too. Michael offered to help with drinks and when Keith declined, pulled up a barstool to keep Keith company while he worked.

The effect of the pill had continued to grow until April felt her pussy might spontaneously climax. She led Victoria to the shower and closed the bathroom door behind them.

"What the fuck was that shit you gave me? I'm drenched. I feel like I'm on the edge of orgasm from dancing. This is nuts."

Victoria grinned. "Ecstasy. Some call it Molly. Unzip me," she said, turning her back.

April did, watching the smooth olive skin reveal itself, feeling a tingling in her pussy. She nudged the dress of Victoria's shoulders. The garment fell in a pile at the tall Latina's feet. Victoria turned. April ran appraising eyes down the woman's body. When Vic reached for April's spaghetti straps, she remained motionless. Now both women faced each other wearing only high-heels and panties.

"I love your big tits," Vic said.

"Show me your pussy," said April, her voice tense.

Victoria slid her panties down. April noted the small strip of pubic hair above the woman's clit. Her outer labia were bald and her inner labia poked through.

Victoria placed a hand behind April's head and pulled her face forward and down. April sank to her knees, her pussy on fire, and slipped a wet tongue into Vic's scorching cunt, tasting pussy for the first time in her life. Vic moaned. April lapped, eager to please, and drank the juice gushing from her Latina lover. Her pussy ached with need when Victoria spoke: "Are you going to fuck Michael?"

"Yes," April groaned.

"Good." She pulled April's mouth tighter. "You'll love it. His cock is huge, long but incredibly thick. Keith will hate what it does to you. Now make me cum."

Victoria lifted a high-heeled foot to the marble counter and held April's mouth firm. Minutes later an obedient April made the hot Latina cum hard. April stood, unsure if it was her turn, but Victoria started the shower.

"Let them know I'll be right out."

April gave a nod and left the bathroom, her desperate pussy clenched like a fist. When she entered the living room, everyone froze. She had no idea why. Maria grinned but Michael, Rudy, and Ernie looked stunned. She faced Keith.

"What's going on? What'd I miss?"

Keith motioned with a wine glass. "Look down, Love."

April lowered her gaze. She was nude except for sheer panties and high-heels. Her erect nipples seemed to reach for the others, aching with a need to be touched. April looked up at her new friends and found only lust staring back.

"Oops."

"Are you drunk, Honey?" Keith asked.

"Yes."

April looked around the room again. She felt the eyes on her moving across her skin like fingertips. When she got to Maria she saw such intense yearning she moved to the girl and stroked her dark hair.

"You are so pretty."

"Thank you," Maria said. "So are you."

April walked around the couch and knelt to put her face close to the Maria's.

"May I kiss you?"

"Please do."

Confusion twisted Keith's face. *April likes girls now?*

Every man in the room watched intently as April leaned over the couch. Maria slipped a tongue out before their lips met and April responded with her own. The boys watched as the girls shared a hot, wet, and erotic kiss. Maria squeezed a naked tit and April moaned and leaned closer. With her other hand Maria caressed another and April lifted her torso and slipped a nipple into Maria's hot mouth.

Rudy moaned a soft, "What the fuck, amigo?"

Ernie nodded in agreement.

Maria took over, alternating between sucking April's nipples and kissing her, working Keith's wife into a state of arousal higher than she'd ever known. At last Maria told April to stand up and Maria pulled the tiny panties down her legs. Keith and the other men saw her bald pussy.

Maria said: "Beautiful," and tugged April closer. The men saw Maria's face disappear between April's legs and April almost lose her balance.

"Oh!" she gasped, "Oh, God!"

She steadied herself by clutching Maria's head. Rudy and Ernie openly rubbed the front of their pants, exchanging incredulous looks. Michael and Keith stared intently. Maria lapped like a puppy, driving April insane, but April's orgasm eluded her. Maria's tongue was a whisper, fliting and darting, teasing and then moving on. She used both hands to spread April's rounded ass cheeks, obscenely displaying her cunt and asshole to the men in the room. April wanted to scream. Her body was on fire. She felt lewd and raunchy and vulgar. Maria pushed her index finger a knuckle deep up April's ass and the poor girl almost cried from overwhelming sensation. Her climax remained just out of reach. April pushed Maria's face away and kissed her gleaming lips.

"I need cock," she croaked.

She looked across the room at Keith and stepped away from Maria, circling the couch in route to her husband. At least, that's what everyone thought, including Keith. As she drew closer it became clear her target was Michael and stunned surprised shook the room. Without a word, she took the man's hand and led him towards the master bedroom.

He considered refusing, for an instant; Keith had been a perfect host. He liked the man. But April was too much woman to deny. Michael wanted her desperately. It was Keith's job to halt this and if he didn't, Michael was blameless. April and Michael disappeared down the hallway. Rudy and Ernie looked at each other and jumped out of their chairs to follow. Keith found himself alone with Maria.

He took a step towards the bedroom.

"Are you sure you want to do that?"

She sat up now, back against the arm of the couch, watching Keith.

"My wife is back there with three men."

"And Victoria, as soon as she steps out of the shower. I can tell you she's safe with those guys. Are you thinking of putting a stop to them?"

Keith tried to look around the corner and down the hall. He rubbed a hand on the back of his neck. Conflict had his brow twisted and his hands nervously fidgeting.

"I…I'm not sure. I'm concerned."

"If you're unsure about stopping them, maybe you want to watch?"

Keith blushed. He was attracted to Maria and now she knew his dirty secret. His face felt hot. He walked to the couch and sat beside her.

"I do, but I feel self-conscious with you guys here. You must think I'm a freak."

"I do, but we're all freaks. Have you watched her before?"

He nodded. "Yes. Twice." He leaned back over the couch to see down the hall but couldn't. "I need to go to April."

"Alright," she said. "Give them a minute. Sit with me. Do you like me?"

"Yes, very much. I think you're gorgeous."

"I find you attractive as well. Can anything happen between us?"

Keith bit his lip. *Fuck I want her.* "No. Not much anyway, and nothing in front of April. We agreed on that rule early on."

She ran her hand over his crotch, felt his semi-erection. She added her other hand and unzipped him, pulling his pudgy penis out. She began to stroke him. He glanced down the hall again.

"I've been with Michael. April is in for a treat. It will be hard for you to watch."

"Why?"

Maria scoffed. "He's a bull."

"I don't understand."

"He's incredibly masculine. The bedroom is his natural habitat. April will respond to him powerfully. He's quiet and reserved but comes alive during sex."

Keith's mouth went dry. "Is he big?"

She felt a surge of blood in his penis as he said it.

"Huge." She displayed his penis. "How did her two lovers compare to you?"

"Bigger."

"Does that excite you?"

"Yes. April loves big ones, too. I get excited when I know she's turned-on."

Maria smiled confidently and tucked Keith back into his pants. She left him unzipped. "Maybe we should go look now? Help me walk, please."

Keith offered her an arm and they moved down the hall slowly. The bedroom door was open only an inch and Keith reached to shove it wide. Maria put a hand on his arm.

"Slowly. Don't disturb them. Open only enough for us to slip in and then push it closed again. Help me."

In moments, they were through the door and inside the room. Keith closed it. Victoria left the bathroom light on and the bedroom was filled with an orange glow. Rudy was naked and stroking his erection in a chair near the bed. Ernie was also nude and masturbating, sitting on the floor near the headboard. Victoria stood at the foot of the bed, a damp towel around her ankles, naked, watching intensely. Keith suspected they'd all done something like this together before.

Michael had April on all fours, head down, ass up, facing Victoria. He was behind her with one knee down, one knee raised, holding her hips and thrusting slowly in and out. One hand guided her hips, the other held a fistful of April's long brown hair, firmly tugging and pulling, steering April where he wanted her. April had her face buried in Keith's pillow, groaning like she underwent surgery.

Keith nudged Maria to move farther down the wall. He wanted to see Michael's penetration of April. Maria smirked and hobbled along and Keith followed.

They cleared the rounded bubble of April's butt and Keith saw the cock fucking his wife. All the air left his lungs. Michael was buried so Keith had no idea of his length, but his girth was just shy of a can of soda. Keith knew he must be wrong, that the dim light and alcohol played tricks, but regardless the man was incredibly thick. His cock neither flexed nor bent as he smoothly pushed and pulled and Keith knew despite the man's size he was hard as stone. A constant river of moans and groans poured from April.

Maria took Keith's hand and moved them closer still. Rudy looked up at them and with a hushed library voice said: "She's already cum once, screaming into that pillow."

Maria leaned close to Keith's ear.

"I've been on the receiving end of that beast," she giggled. "You think you have an ocean liner buried inside you but you love it all the same. The darkest moment of your life is when he pulls it out. The emptiness slaps you in the face. Your pussy aches for it again every day. Far better a woman never meet that cock than to face going on with life without it."

Keith watched his lovely bride. She was a fish on a hook, wriggling, turning and twisting as the shank of beef within her turned her mind inside out. Michael murmured soft commands too low for Keith to hear, but he was too mesmerized by his wife's behavior to care. She rotated her ass and clenched her pussy. Her chest expanded and contracted as she struggled to get enough air. Her beautiful tits were mashed to the sides as April squeezed the pillow tight and her long hair was spread in a tousled mess like a blanket. He watched his girl, his sweetheart, the love of his lifetime, fuck another and thought she'd never looked more lovely. His penis rose and protruded through his open zipper. Maria saw the movement and thought about stroking him again but remembered what he'd said about their rules.

April had pushed up from the mattress and was now on hands and knees. Her plump tits bounced and swung in circles as Michael fucked her harder. Her back bowed. Keith read her body perfectly; Michael was driving her crazy. The man stroked faster still, holding her hips with both hands, and April was a docile and submissive breeding bitch. Her eyes were squeezed shut as she savored every solid inch he gave her.

Unknown to Keith, powerful chemicals flowed through her bloodstream, lifting her to a surreal experience not of this world. April felt herself wrapped around the cock an oyster around a pearl. Her purpose at this moment was to gratify the cock, tease the cock, coax the cock to disgorge its seed into her hot and heaving womb. The fleshy spike moving within her was a bringer of life. She craved the load contained within those corpulent balls. She needed it. She felt universally connected to all women at that moment. Michael reached under and caressed her full breasts and the sensitivity rocked her. Her nipples yowled at the contact sending a burst of pleasure racing through her body. Her tight asshole pulsed and contracted.

She felt her body begin to buckle and contract again. Another orgasm ripped her to pieces and she held on and rode it out. Color and light fired through her brain and electricity tightened every muscle she had, which focused her entire being on the foreign object pummeling her. She screamed and pounded the bed with a fist before collapsing head down again.

Keith heard her sob under Michael's relentless pounding. His stomach flipped and then filled with ice water. This man controlled his wife by owning her pussy. Worse, she wanted him to have control over her. Keith knew if he ordered her to stop at this moment she would not. She would continue to give herself to Michael, instantly obeying anything he told her to do.

When April finally looked up and realized her husband was present, she saw Keith's eyes wide and haunted, his face drained of blood.

"Baby," she called softly, extending a hand to him. "Oh, Christ."

Keith stepped closer and took her hand and she squeezed so hard she hurt him. Michael changed angles and April cried out in pleasure and Keith held her hand as she climaxed again, shouting nonsense before collapsing to the bed. Only Michael's hands on her hips kept her pussy in the air as he hammered her little pussy.

He pushed her flat and crawled farther up her body, never breaking rhythm. He used his feet to spread her ankles and Rudy and Ernie leaned over to look up between her legs at her penetration. Maria and Victoria leaned too. Everyone except Keith knew what was coming next. Michael held her small waist with both hands and began dropping his hips to drive his cock as deep as possible. April tossed her head wildly, penetrated beyond anything she'd ever known. Michael sucked lungs full of air and pumped faster and, too late, Keith finally understood.

Michael roared as searing hot sperm ejaculated inside April like a firehose. Over and over the man flexed his ass and drove his hips and Keith realized each was a new bolt of frothy semen. Michael pumped a seeming gallon of jizz, flooding her small uterus and vagina until splashing sounds filled the room every time his hips crashed forward. Keith thought the man's climax lasted an eternity and April begged for every drop.

"Look at your wife taking it," Maria whispered. "Look how she wants his cum."

Michael's thrusts finally slowed and he laid his body on top of April's.

"That…was…the hottest thing I've ever seen," Victoria murmured.

Nobody moved. No one else spoke. The only sound was Michael trying hard to catch his breath. Maria nudged Keith and jerked a chin towards the door. Dumbfounded, he turned and shuffled out. Rudy, Ernie, and Victoria followed. Victoria left the towel on the ground and shut the door behind them.

In the living room, the boys dropped into chairs, Maria took one end of the couch and Keith took the other. Victoria, still nude, curled up on Maria's lap.

"That was crazy," Ernie said. "Like, Michael is a God and shit."

Rudy grinned. "For real. Jesus. I've seen Michael fuck a bitch before but not like that. Never like that. He fucking loves that bitch."

Victoria and Maria murmured to each other too low for anyone to hear. Keith stared at the coffee table. Fifteen minutes later, a soft and distinctly feminine moan floated through the room followed by a low rhythmic thumping against the bedroom wall.

Ernie grinned and Rudy said: "Dude is fucking her again already."

"Keith," Victoria said. "You and Maria are the only ones dressed. Why don't you join us? Take off your clothes. You, too, Maria."

"Help me get undressed," Maria said. Vic leaned over to help her undress.

Keith was reluctant but sitting clothed in a room full of naked seemed too odd. He grabbed his drink and finished it in one gulp and then stripped. His penis was partially aroused and Maria stared at it, which he loved. He moved to the bar and poured himself a double whiskey and asked for drink orders. Everyone wanted refills.

The soft moans and quiet cries of pleasure through the wall was too much and Victoria and Maria started making out. Ernie and Rudy watched them and masturbated. Keith listened to Michael drive April wild again and his penis rose to full erection. Maria stared at it while she kissed Victoria.

Soon April screamed as her pleasure exploded and not long after Michael rumbled a long groan. Keith knew at that moment the man inseminated April with another massive load.

Victoria and Maria continued enjoying each other while the men watched. Keith downed his drink and fixed another. His buzz was strong and he suspected he should stop but knew he wouldn't. Not in this situation.

After some time, they heard the bedroom door open and footsteps come up the hallway. Michael, nude and sporting a huge hanging phallus, entered the living room. Keith saw the length of the man and a chill raced through him as that meant all that sperm was injected directly into April's womb. Michael dropped into the only open chair, avoiding everyone's eyes, and turned to watch the girls, his glittering meat-hose hanging off the chair between his legs. Keith stared at it. Although made profoundly uncomfortable by the thought, he had to admit it was a beautiful dick.

Keith debated going to check on his wife. Most likely she was deep asleep and after all the alcohol she'd consumed, that was probably best. On the other hand, he wondered how she looked and how she felt. As always he felt the urge to examine her, to see the evidence of her infidelities. If she was awake she may want to see him. For long minutes, he sat undecided. A scuff against carpet made everyone turn towards the bedroom.

April was there, standing at the head of the hall, balanced by a hand against the bar, surveying the living room and everyone in it. Her body was covered with sweat and her hair a terrible mess. A long white trail of sperm ran down her inner thigh.

Keith was about to speak when April left the bar and walked across the room. He knew she was coming to him so he sat up straight. When she turned at the coffee table and went to Ernie, Keith's mind went numb. His mouth dropped open. His head tilted to one side in utter disbelief. She held out her hand and Ernie grinned like a fool. He took the offered hand and followed her towards the bedroom. His penis bobbed as he walked but at this moment April no longer cared if her lover was big. His dick was hard and so needed emptying.

Keith covered his face with both hands. His penis pulsed, standing straight up. He glanced at Maria and her eyes were riveted still to his erection and he considered breaking the rules and fucking her, but Victoria between her legs made things awkward.

Apparently, April left the bedroom door open this time because the sounds of sex were obvious. The bed squeaked and Ernie growled and April urged him on, telling him to fuck her hard. Keith was stunned when his wife climaxed again. Ernie told April to take his cum as he shot her full and soon after sheepishly rejoined the group in the living room.

Minutes later April reappeared and led Rudy away.

This time Keith gave them a minute or two and followed. Rudy had April on her back and she had her arms and legs wrapped around the olive-skinned man. He fucked her hard, like he knew he'd never fuck a woman this gorgeous again and wanted her to remember him, and Keith was again staggered when later his wife cried out in earth-shaking orgasm. Keith left the room before they noticed him.

Back in the living room he discovered Ernie was gone. They all got comfortable and listed to the sounds of sex from the bedroom until Rudy appeared. He dressed quickly and said goodnight, shaking Keith's hand like crazy and thanking him.

Once Rudy was gone, Maria asked: "What are the sleeping arrangements?"

Victoria answered: "This couch makes out into a bed. I say you and I sleep here and Michael and Keith join April in the master bed."

Michael stood and hugged the two women and headed down the hall.

Keith stood frozen. *Share a bed with the man that fucked my wife?*

Maria spoke: "Keith, if you want to suck Michael's cock, he'll let you."

Keith stepped back like he'd been slapped. "What?"

"A lot of guys want to suck his dick after they see it. I don't blame them; I know I did." Victoria chuckled and Maria continued. "Michael doesn't mind. He's actually flattered by it. You don't need permission first, either. I don't know what's going to happen in there but I just thought you should know he's cool like that."

"Yeah, um, thanks but I'll pass."

"Whatever."

Keith helped open the couch into a bed and found extra pillows. Once he had the girls ready to sleep, he stood there.

"Thank you for everything," Victoria purred. "What a great night. I know I'll never forget it and I'm sure you won't either."

Maria giggled.

When he could stall no longer, he walked the long march to the bedroom.

April was in the middle of the bed with Michael behind her. Keith climbed in and spread the covers over them all, up to their chins. He lay on his side, facing April. When his head hit the pillow, he discovered she was awake and gazing at him, their faces less than a foot apart.

She smiled weakly, clearly exhausted. "Move closer," she asked. "Hold me."

He noticed her pupils were huge but scooted close enough the front of their bodies touched all the way down, He rested his head on her large breasts. She wrapped her arms around his head and shoulders. He nuzzled closer. Her warm breath blew across an ear. After a while they changed positions, this time April snuggled up to him and he wrapped her in his arms, both too tired to sleep.

"Did you fuck Maria?" she muttered.

"No, Baby."

"Good. Hug me."

He squeezed tighter. Her body rocked some and he thought she was trying for a more comfortable position but then she softly groaned and bit her bottom lip. Keith was confused for a moment and then understood; behind her Michael was once again pushing deep. Keith loosened his arms but April stopped him.

"No. Don't go. Hold me, Honey. Squeeze me."

Keith tightened his grip, feeling the weight and strength of Michael behind her. April moaned and closed her eyes but quickly opened them again, finding his.

"He's…fucking…me…Keith," she said, her eyes dreamy with pleasure. "Baby, I love it so much." Her eyelids fluttered and she licked her lips, moving her butt back a few inches each time Michael thrust. "Keith, he's going to make me cum again. I can't take it. Hold me, Baby."

Keith held his wife as Michael fucked her. The skin between her eyebrows crinkled each time the man pushed his cock deep and her hot breath warmed his throat. He saw her eyeballs rolling around under her lids and gathered a sense of what she must be feeling.

"Do you love his cock, April?"

"I do, Baby," she murmured. "More than James. Michael's sooooo thick. I'm forced to cum. I can't help it. He rips them from me. It's the most amazing thing."

She squeezed her eyes and Keith felt her drift away, back to that place where her body contorts and convulses and a mind-expanding orgasm tears through her. Her brow slowly knotted as Michael continued his smooth in and out. Soon she was breathing deep, her mouth wide open.

Watching Michael's effect on her was intense. He held his wife as another man fucked her, driving her relentlessly towards climax, and it was almost too much to bear.

Her hands were tucked down the front of her body and she felt Keith's erection bump them so on instinct she held on and began jerking with short strokes.

Keith watched his wife's face as she climbed. At last her head curled back and April screamed as her body flailed, sandwiched between the two men.

The stimulation was too much and Keith spurted all over her hands and stomach. White light filled his head and he heard himself gasp and moan. Another deep moan intruded on top of his and he understood Michael was once again filling April with cum. April was pressed between two men simultaneously climaxing and she wailed in pleasure as another smaller orgasm shook her. When it ended, they all remained where they were. April finally fell asleep, utterly spent and Michael's deep breathing followed not long after. Eventually sleep claimed Keith too.

They awoke well after noon. The girls were gone, the sofa-bed made. Michael was gone leaving only a brief note thanking April for the most fantastic night of his life and his cell number. Groggy and stupid, they ate a couple power bars, drank a gallon of water, and crawled back into bed. They snuggled as close as possible and fell back to sleep.

They awoke famished. Neither said anything about the night they'd shared and they gave each other time to organize thoughts and feelings. They ate at the hotel restaurant and changed into beach gear and aimed for the nude beach, ready to sweat out the alcohol from the night before.

This beach was cleaner and more populated than Playalinda, although the ratio of single men was higher. That suited April just fine and her head was on a pivot all day. Keith noted there was no sole type for her; April liked almost every kind of man. They found a spot between two groups of single men and spread their blanket and dropped to the sand. They napped holding hands and facing the blue Miami sky.

April woke first and let Keith sleep while she wandered down to the water to swim. Up on the blanket and inside her purse, her cell buzzed with an incoming call. When no one answered, the caller tried again. On the third try, Keith woke and fished her phone from the purse to see if the call was an emergency. The number was blocked so Keith knew it was a sales call and dropped the phone back into her purse, annoyed at being awakened. The phone hit something hard and plastic. Keith looked to see what it was and after a second of confusion, gasped.

April's disk of birth control pills lay staring up at him and pills for the last three days remined in the wrapper. Today's pill remained as well. Last night had been completely unprotected.

"Holy fuck!"

Faces all over the beach turned to look at his outburst. He grabbed the disk to double and triple check but the truth was there; April had stopped taking pills days ago.

"Holy fuck!" he yelled again.

A glance at the water showed April on her way back to the blanket. He held up the dispenser as she drew near.

"What. The. Hell?"

She hung her head. "I know, terrible, right?"

She wrung the water from her long hair and dropped to her knees.

Keith's heart hammered. "Why, April? Are you trying to get pregnant with another man?"

Her face contorted. "Keith! Of course not. I stopped taking them after we had our baby-talk back in Orlando. I was finished with other men after James. Why do you think I turned down Cameron? That man was gorgeous *and* he would have been my first black guy. I wanted him but I thought I'd had enough."

She lay on her back and continued; "This trip has opened our world and brought us closer than ever before and I thought conceiving a baby with you while on it would be perfection. I didn't plan on last night. Whatever that pill Victoria gave me sent me into the stratosphere. I planned on stopping by a pharmacy today for the morning-after pill because it is literally the morning after. How can you worry I'd want another man's baby? You think me capable of that?"

"Victoria gave you drugs?"

"Yes, in the ladies' room last night. Amazing stuff but sure messed up my plans. Answer my question."

"I'm sorry. I saw the pills and panicked. This trip has been amazing but it has also been emotionally exhausting. I've been put through the ringer. It was a stupid thing to say. I apologize."

She reached up and kissed him. "I guess I can understand that. Baby, I would never, ever cheat on you like that. A baby? That's over the top, Honey. I'd have to be a supreme asshole bitch."

"What drugs? Why didn't you tell me?"

"I wanted to see if you'd notice me acting differently, plus I wanted you straight while I was high. I worried she'd give you some too. I thought one of us should at least act a little responsibly."

"How was it?"

She gazed into his eyes intensely. "A-ma-zing. Mind altering. I'm exhausted but I want more. I want to do it again. I want you to do it, too. I want us to make love on it. I think it was ecstasy but I'm not sure. Did you get Maria or Victoria's number?"

"No."

"Good boy. I guess I'll have to text Michael then. Just to find out what it was."

They kissed again and April laid on her back. She closed her eyes. Keith was about to do the same but the beads of water scattered across her skin accentuated her curves and caught his eye. Her tanned skin gave her a healthy glow. Her nipples were hard from the breeze drying the water. He started at her big tits and ran his eyes down her body until her reached her bald pussy.

Michael is in her, he thought. *Three times. Rudy and Ernie, too.*

His balls tingled.

And now she's completely unprotected.

His penis began to swell. He scanned the beach nervously, afraid someone would see, afraid someone would read his perverted mind and know.

Hundreds of millions, billions of sperm, swimming inside her right now.

Blood surged and just like that he was growing.

Why does the thought excite me so much? I yell at her about it but deep down, it makes me hot as fuck.

A droplet of water ran off her body and between her legs. She flicked it away with a hand and touched her pussy lips, tapping lightly, making sure everything was tucked neatly away. A milky drop of sperm oozed between her tight lips and trickled towards her asshole. Keith saw cloudy swirls contained within. He moaned.

Oh, God.

April opened her eyes, saw where he was looking.

"Is that Michael running out of me or seawater?"

Keith's throat was so constricted he could barely answer. "Michael."

She spotted his erection poking up from his lap. "Baby? Are you turned-on because I'm not on the pill and he's in there?"

"Yes." *I'm doomed.*

"Why?"

"I don't fully know. God, this is humiliating."

"I thought you were angry?"

"I was. I am. Fuck, I don't know, Baby."

April studied her husband's face and then glanced around the beach. She slipped a hand down her stomach and spread her labia wide open.

"You want to eat my pussy or have you moved beyond that these days?"

"We'd get arrested, but no, I'm not in the mood after so many men."

"So…many…men," she repeated, teasing.

"You are too good at this game. This is nuts."

"Right now, or the life we're living?"

"The life. Will it be like this when we get back to Vegas?"

"Good question. Could cause serious problems there. We can blame it on the vacation and save it for when we leave town."

He nodded slowly. "How do you feel right now, April? What did last night do to you? I know you're exhausted but beyond that; what are your feelings?"

She thought for a moment. "I'm worried about getting pregnant. I'm giddy about so many new and sexy lovers. I'm thrilled you are by my side. I'm really, really happy. My life has never been better."

He looked at her spread pussy.

"You love it, don't you, Keith? Michael came in my unprotected cunt and you love it. Does it excite you as much that I took Rudy and Ernie too?

"No."

She pursed her lips. "So, only Michael…because he's big?"

"Yeah. I like it more because I know you like it more. I'm a freak."

"Baby, so am I." She weighed her next words carefully before speaking. She wanted to invite Michael over for another tryst but worried it was too soon. She studied her husband's face and decided against it.

"Lay on your stomach," she suggested. "Let's nap in the sun together."

He nodded again and with a final look at her swollen pussy, lay next to her.

She may have decided to skip Michael for now but her mind raced ahead. She imagined him inside her again and her pussy felt achingly empty.

I fucked Ryan with the intention of telling Keith. I sucked David's cock knowing Keith would return and catch me. They were different ways of playing our same game together.

She thought again about Michael's thick cock moving inside her.

What if I fuck Michael and don't tell Keith at all?

The thought shamed her and guilt rushed in to crush her. Keith was not worthy of such thinking. He'd given her anything she wanted, sometimes at great personal cost.

Am I really so selfish? What a bitch.

Nevertheless, the thought lingered as she drifted off to sleep.

After the beach, they grabbed a late dinner and crashed back at the hotel, watching movies in bed. *Ant-man* had just ended when April grabbed Keith's arm and exclaimed, 'Goddamn it!"

"What? What's wrong?"

"We never visited the pharmacy! I need to get that pill. What's wrong with us?"

"Alright, Honey, we'll go first thing tomorrow."

The next movie started and after a while April relaxed.

All Keith could think about was all that semen inside his wife, swimming freely. After a few minutes he pushed April onto her back and opened her robe.

She'd showered when they got back to the hotel so Keith kissed a trail down her flat stomach to her pussy. April put both hands on his head. She always felt an extra wicked thrill if Keith ate her after she'd fucked someone else, like she was the ultimate princess, and after Michael this was especially true. Keith was a masterful cunnilinguist and April spread her legs and enjoyed his tongue fully. Shower or not, Keith encountered evidence of others. He ignored it, savoring the cries of pleasure his wife made, and once he made her orgasm he moved up her body and pushed his penis deep. Her pussy enveloped him smoothly and all at once and Keith lasted almost no time at all before adding his to the many loads she already carried.

The next day Keith mentioned a playoff football game he wanted to watch and April said she'd use that time to go shopping and stop by the drug store. They kissed at the hotel room door and Keith made sure she had the other room key.

Once she was gone he got comfortably ensconced in the couch. He had beer and pretzels handy, shut the blinds, dimmed the lights, engaged stereo surround sound, sat his cell close by in case April called or text, rubbed his hands together, and laughed diabolically.

"Go Raiders!" he yelled.

At that moment, April sat outside a Walgreens, wrestling with her conscience. In her purse, she had three doses of Mifepristone. Before last night she would have already washed the thing down but Keith made love to her last night and that complicated things. She might be pregnant with Rudy or Ernie or Michael's baby, but she now might be pregnant with hers and Keith's. She held her head in her hands and stared at the sidewalk. Her stomach churned.

The risk is too high. The odds are against Keith and I. Michael alone filled me four times. I should just take this and be done with it.

She remembered the last time Michael claimed her. Keith lay dead to the world, asleep in the bed next to her as Michael plumbed her depths with strong, sure strokes. She'd successfully covered her scream when she climaxed and he'd buried his face in her hair when he shot her full.

Keith knows about three. The fourth was all mine.

The fourth had been different for April. By then she'd developed feelings for Michael, as women do. They'd kissed with passion and genuine connection. She was sure he'd felt it too.

That's why he slipped out so quickly before dawn. To avoid Keith and I together.

She rubbed her lower belly.

This pill flushes them all out.

She thought about the men she'd had last night and felt deliciously naughty. An idea popped into her head.

If I fucked Michael one last time, that would get flushed out too.

She watched people walk by on their way someplace else.

That would be cheating. But would it? Was it cheating when I fucked Michael in the same bed next to Keith? Is it my fault he was too drunk and tired to awaken?

She knew she was rationalizing but didn't much care. The idea of seeing him one last time had her heart racing. She pulled her phone from her purse and text Michael a message.

The Lyft ride was inexpensive as Michael lived only a few blocks from downtown Miami. She met him at Simpson park and followed him to his high-rise at The Palace. He wore sandals and white linen pants and shirt and took her breath when she saw him. He smiled broadly and kissed her deeply. She'd worn a simple cotton green skirt and lime top and worried she wasn't pretty enough, but his smile dissipated all that.

Michael introduced her to his roommate, Israel, and then aimed her towards his bedroom. She nervously tugged at the loose skin on her hand, deeply questioning her decision to come. Realizing she'd made a mistake, she turned to tell him. She heard the dead-bolt click. The desire in his eyes stopped the words in her throat.

"I will never grow accustomed to your beauty," he said, his Latin accent giving her shivers. He came forward and took her into his arms and they kissed again.

After a minute, April pulled away to sink to her knees. She tugged the drawstring and his baggy pants fell to his ankles and his heavy manhood swayed. She remembered how good he felt inside and moaned lightly. He stroked her hair.

"All in good time," he said.

April opened her mouth and began to suck the sweetest cock she'd ever known. She ran her tongue around the crown and wiggled it into the small opening at the tip. She sucked hard, denting her cheeks, and then relaxed her throat and pushed as many inches as she could towards the back. She held him there, unhurried, savoring the hot pulse of his heartbeat against her tongue. Her hands came up to cup his huge balls and softly roll them around inside their skin bag. One large testicles in each hand, she compared him to Keith before she could stop herself.

Twice the size and easily more than twice the weight.

She felt guilt for such an unworthy thought but the knowledge also sent a thrill through her. Michael was so manly, so masculine. He had a powerful male presence. She slipped his cock from her mouth and went down to lick those virile balls.

He had been so eager to be inside her last night they'd skipped almost all foreplay. He welcomed her oral worship of the cock she'd fallen in love with. He grew slowly but steadily and soon she had a lance protruding from his pelvis. In the light, face to face, she scarcely believed she'd taken the thing so many times. She understood much better why her pussy was tender. He pulled off his shirt, slipped of his sandals, and stepped out of his pants. He lifted her to her feet and with swift, gentle movements had her nude in moments.

To see her now was to see her for the first time. She squirmed under his intense gaze but she loved it. No longer clouded by alcohol, drugs, darkness, or haste, he scrutinized every inch, his throbbing cock hardening further, now deep red and purple. April was dying to touch it again but loved his eyes on her too much to move.

Finally, he took her hand and led her to the bed. Her legs felt weak. He backed her onto it and followed, crawling on his knees between her legs. More and more her eyes left his to fasten themselves to his turgid weapon. Looking directing down the barrel like this she was mortified by the thickness. She impulsively reached down and discovered her fingers did not meet. Not even close. An image of her hand around Keith's penis showed her thumb atop her index finger to the first knuckle. She moaned.

"Please," she breathed. "Don't tease me. Don't make me wait."

His grin melted her. "I couldn't if I tried. I've thought of nothing else since I met you."

She wrapped both hands behind his neck and fell back, taking his head with her. His chest mashed her tits and the head of his dick grazed her labia. Her hips rose, trying to capture his cock. She sought his shaft and, finding the massive cannon, rubbed the head to spilt her pussy lips and wet it. He felt the furnace of her opening and nudged forward and her labia blossomed around him and enveloped the head in searing wetness. He pushed again, encountering the same resistance he had the night before. He used his body weight and his strength to forge ahead, forcing her tunnel to expand and accept him. No longer hidden behind the mask of drugs, April experienced a penetration like nothing she'd ever felt before.

"Fucking Christ, Michael, you're huge."

"Same cock as last night, Love. Try to relax. I'll go slow. You're certainly wet enough. I think you like me."

They kissed and Michael made small in and out movements, getting his cock slick, pushing a little deeper every time. April gasped and then gasped again, louder. He loved the absurd grip her cunt had on him. Minutes passed as he steadily worked himself deeper. At last his balls touched her sphincter and she groaned with a welcome discomfort.

"That's it. You have all of me."

April exhaled air she was unaware she held. She brought her feet up behind him and crossed her ankles. They kissed again.

"Fuck me, Michael," she whispered, and circled his neck with her arms.

He started slow but too much passion seethed between them. Soon the bed bounced, thumping the wall. Michael rolled her on top and let her ride him, watching as she mauled her own lovely tits and lifted her hair.

In many ways, this was her first time with him. Huge chunks of last night were a hedonistic haze. His steel cock inside her was solid and immovable and she drove her pussy up and down furiously. When she came, she screamed and fell forward.

He gave her no time to recover. He rolled her on her back again and slipped both hands under to cup her ass, maximizing his penetration. Her pussy milked him with quivering waves. He felt her tighten around him and her face get serious and thought she might cum again so he moved a finger over and slid one knuckle deep in her ass. She tried to move away, for half a second, until she realized her anal penetration combined with his massive cock filling her cunt was the most amazing thing she'd ever experienced. She urged him on, telling him to fuck her harder and faster, until she bit his neck hard and orgasmed like an earthquake.

His penis swelled as she was coming down and she planted both hands on his ass and pulled him deep to shoot. He unloaded an ocean of sperm far up in her. They lay silent a long time, cherishing the entanglement of their sweaty bodies, and then began kissing. The kissing became more passionate and Michael surprised them both by growing mostly hard again.

This time they made slow and deliberate love. They knew they'd never see each other again, or at least the chance was microscopic, so they wanted to remember every second spent together. Much later, when she climaxed it was drawn out, lasting a long time while he continued to move in and out of her. His climax was surprisingly powerful and she felt a thud when the first blast of sperm hit her uterine wall.

After that they caught their breath and chatted, discussing Miami but not the future, feeling the moment drain away. She dressed and left him in bed.

She waited for the Lyft downstairs and checked her phone. Nothing from Keith. She was home-safe. She told the driver to take her to the nearest mall and as she shopped the weight of what she'd done began to press down on her. She found a lady's room and drew the Mifepristone from her purse. She stared at the little white pill on her palm. She turned the water on. Several moments passed.

When I get home. That way Keith can see me take it too.

She put the pill in her skirt pocket. She knew the real reason she was reluctant to take the pill was to keep Michael inside as long as possible, but she would not allow herself to think about that.

Keith will feel better if he sees me take it.

At the thought of her husband she withdrew her phone and sent him a text saying she loved him and hoped his game went well.

"Raiders up by ten!" he sent back.

She smiled and put her phone away. She remembered Michael's fat cock in her mouth, gagging her, making it hard to breathe, dominating and overwhelming her and she longed to have that cock in her mouth again.

She returned to the hotel room and discovered Keith had ordered dinner delivered. She told him all about her shopping day but said nothing of Michael.

Keith talked about the exciting football game. They ate and she felt herself reconnect to the man she loved, even as her pussy tingled with the memory of Michael's enormous phallus. After dinner, she drew the pill from her pocket and showed it to Keith.

"I hesitated because we made love last night. I might carry our baby already."

His face went serious. "I didn't think about that."

They pondered together, staring at the pill on her open hand.

"No, the risk is too high. You must take it. That's my vote."

She nodded and washed the pill down with a glass of wine. She said she wanted to shower the day off and he turned to Sportscenter. She lathered and scrubbed and examined herself for any sign of her indiscretion and once satisfied, joined Keith in front of the television for a movie before bed.

They both slept like rocks.

For two days, they were absolutely the very best friends. Sex was pushed into the background after their last adventure. They saw sights, ate when hungry, slept when tired. They shopped and laughed and laughed and laughed. April was especially attentive and Keith noticed but when he asked her why she told him she was grateful for all the sacrifices he'd made on this strip.

At last their attention came back around to the trip home and Keith suggested they just catch a plane straight to Vegas.

"We'll be home in five hours."

"That sounds fabulous."

They spent their last night in Miami and then raised a toast to Tartarus.

"The club that *was* better than any Vegas club," Keith said.

"We'll never forget that place," April agreed. "Or the night that followed."

Their plane touched down at McCarran smoothly. They collected their luggage, hailed a cab, and headed for home, both too exhausted to do anything other than drop their bags and collapse on the bed to stare at the ceiling.

"What a fucking amazing trip," Keith said.

"It was," April agreed. "We turned our world upside-down. Can we even go back to our old life?"

"No, no way. How could something so small and safe ever satisfy us now?"

"So, are we going to continue some of the things we discovered on the road?"

Keith hesitated before answering. "You mean; *Can I still fuck other men?*"

April snorted. "Yeah, I guess I do. If that's how you want to word it. We talked briefly about 'vacation rules,' but never discussed details. At the time, I honestly thought I might be over it but now it's stronger than ever."

"If people knew it might hurt our careers, and what about kids? You would need to come off birth control."

"Any man would need to use a condom."

"True. I hate those things but I wouldn't be the one wearing them, and any man *would* slap one on for the chance to fuck you."

"Oh they would, would they?"

"Fuck yes. You're my wife and I'd wear one if I had to." He rolled over and kissed her and then rolled on top, his legs outside hers. "So let's throw some ideas around; no friends, no coworkers."

"No locals. Vegas brings in people from all over the world so there will always be a fresh supply."

Keith laughed. "Fresh supply?"

"Yes. I told you I'm horny all the time now. I think about sex seven-twenty-four."

"How will you find the hung ones?"

She touched a finger to her lips, thoughtful. "Good question. Dancing with them will help. No nude beaches in the desert. Maybe you can follow them into the restroom, or just ask them."

"Way too creepy. Maybe we can visit a sex club?"

"Oh! I like that idea. That sounds fun regardless. We don't have to return to work until Monday morning. Let's hit a sex club this weekend. Amazing how just a few weeks ago that sentences would have been an impossibility."

He kissed her again and rolled off. "I'll call Gary and let him know we're home and thank him for getting the mail and watering the plants. We should take him to dinner or get him movie tickets."

"Okay."

Keith found his phone to dial Gary and April began to unpack.

An hour later April stepped out of the shower, wrapped a towel around her wet hair, and headed for the kitchen, craving a beer. She opened the fridge and then the beer, dropped the top in the trash, and turned around to head back to the bedroom, pulling hard on the bottle.

Gary stood across the room gawking at her.

Her eyes went big. "What the hell?" she spat, lowering the beer and trying to cover tits and pussy with arms.

"I'm so sorry, Ape. Keith is in the pisser. I got here fifteen minutes ago and he was telling me all about your trip. I thought you knew I was here."

April backed out of the living room. "I was in the shower and didn't hear you guys. I'm so embarrassed. Tell Keith he's in big trouble!"

Gary laughed. "Will do."

He tried his best to keep his eyes on hers but fuck that, he wanted to see everything. When she'd first entered the room, his eyes had immediately gone to her bald pussy. He knew he'd take that vision to the grave. Her body was even better than he'd imagined and he'd done a lot of imagining over the years.

She turned to walk into the bedroom again, sooner than she had to, showing Gary her round ass and her bare slit from behind.

Bloody fucking hell, he thought. *I'd fuck that woman to death and not care she's married to my best friend.* He immediately felt shitty.

Keith was the best man he knew. He'd told Keith his feelings about April after meeting her for the first time and that was before she got in shape and learned to dress and style her hair and make-up. He could see then she was stunning. Now she was world-class gorgeous.

April closed the bedroom, smirking. Gary's gaze thrilled her. He was a good-looking man; taller than her husband, light brown hair and expressive eyes. At first his pale skin had made him look unhealthy but over the years she'd come to like it.

I wonder if his dick is bigger than Keith's?

She pulled the towel off and began drying her hair.

I'm such a bitch. I compare every guy to my husband now.

She tossed the towel on the bed.

That makes sense though; that's the first penis I met. That's the penis that took my virginity. That's the penis I'll be spending the rest of my life with. No wonder I measure everyone else to Keith.

Keith came into the bathroom to check on her but did not mention the encounter with Gary. She thought about telling him but something kept her silent.

If Gary said nothing, why should I?

They chatted for a bit and Keith mentioned Gary was out in the living room.

"Okay, thanks, I'll come out and say hello in a few minutes."

Keith gave her a peck on the cheek and left.

April put on a baggy T-shirt with the arms cut off and loose shorts. She turned the mirrors in the bathroom to look at herself from every angle and then ran tests on lifting her arms and bending over, noting what she revealed and how much. She smiled.

I am a changed woman. Gary thinks I'm pretty. I think I might play with the man.

She applied light make-up and joined the men in the living room. As usual, she picked the end of the couch opposite Gary, her back against the arm. From her experiments in the mirror she knew her husband saw only T-shirt and shorts but with a twist of her butt she could flash Gary her smooth pussy and if she lifted her beer just right he'd see down her sleeve hole to her tits. Warmth spread from her lower tummy down into her pelvis.

Gary asked a million questions about the trip and they told him all the pedestrian activities, leaving anything erotic out of the conversation. In time, Keith went for fresh beers and April innocently shifted her ass causing the loose pant leg to billow and open. Gary took half a second to notice and then he was staring at April's cunt. When he glanced at her face she was fiddling with her cuticles, oblivious, so he stared some more.

April loved his eyes on her.

He's wanted me for so long. I wonder what he sees down there.

She giggled on the inside.

I wonder if I can make him hard in front of Keith?

Keith returned and sat a new beer in front of Gary and conversation started up again. As April and Keith shared details of their trip, she carefully repositioned her legs and arms, giving Gary glimpses of pussy, tits, and nipples. Sure enough, she saw the bulge in his lap grow.

Eventually time caught up and Keith said he was tired. Gary said goodnight and gave Keith a hug and a back-slap and then turned to April. Keith headed for the bedroom. April watched him go and then spoke: "Whatever happened to that girl you were dating? Helen, right?"

Gary spread his arms and April stepped inside them.

"I'm still seeing her."

"Getting serious? It's been a long time."

"Pretty serious, yes. I asked her to marry me six months ago. She said yes."

"Congrats."

April brought her body up against his. Her abdomen pressed his crotch and she felt the solid outline of an erection.

Nice.

They hugged just slightly longer than was usual or appropriate and Gary covered by saying he was happy they were home safe. Her body felt like magic against his. He knew she probably felt his hard-on but didn't care.

Let her know I think she's hot.

April gave it right back, leaning into him, pressing her body firmly against his all the way down. He held the embrace for several heartbeats and then broke, kissing her cheek and saying goodnight. She walked him to the door, fully aware he stared at her ass the whole way.

She locked the door behind him.

Keith was already in bed reading the news on his Kindle. She pulled off her T-shirt and stepped out of her shorts and slipped under the covers naked.

"So refresh my memory," she said after a few minutes. "The last time we talked about me pulling a Ryan is not so much that I did it behind your back, but that you felt threatened and foolish. Am I right?"

He set his Kindle on the bed. "Why? You thinking about fucking someone behind my back? Did you just have sex with Gary?"

She chuckled. "Of course not, but I told you I think about sex all the time. What if something spontaneous were to happen? It's not practical that I always do it in front of you, not to mention some guys will not be okay with you there watching, but what about something impulsive? What if I'm out shopping and I meet someone, like with Tammy? Can I pursue it if I tell you everything after? We can fuck like rabbits when I get home and spill my guts. Maybe I can even text you while it is happening? Imagine getting pictures. That's hot. We need to keep the element of surprise."

"This makes me uneasy, Honey."

"I understand, but can't you just trust me? I swear I'll never leave you and especially not over sex."

Keith studied her face. "Did you? Did you already fuck someone?"

"Yes."

Keith's blood ran cold. "Who? When?"

She decided on a half-truth, knowing it would alleviate much of her lingering guilt. She knew she was rationalizing but did it anyway. "Remember that night in bed with me, you, and

Michael? You held me while he fucked me a third time. God, that was amazing. Anyway, we all fell asleep but he woke up an hour later and took me *again*. You were out; too much booze, I guess. We tried to be quiet and you never woke, but I've wondered ever since; was that cheating? Did that violate our rule? I'd just fucked him in front of you. There's so much gray."

Keith weighed her words. "I hesitate to just give you carte blanche, April."

"Baby," she purred. "It's just sex. Nothing is going to happen while you're not there that won't happen right in front of you. I feel like we're cutting this sexy life in half. We've discovered something amazing but you only want to take sips while I want to guzzle. Life is short."

He groaned and stared at the ceiling. When he didn't answer, she snuggled up under an arm and laid her head on his chest.

"What are you reading? Did we miss any big news events while we were away?"

Tammy's face lit up when April entered the store.

"Wow, girl! You look amazing. All tan and fit and relaxed. Must have been a great trip."

"It was. Phenomenal."

The women hugged and then Tammy marched April towards a dressing room. April spoke about the trip, hitting all the obvious highlights. As they entered the back area she lowered her voice. "Tammy, my husband and I are going to a Vegas sex club this weekend, just to check it out, and I have no idea what to wear. Have you ever gone?"

Tammy leaned in close as she guided April into a dressing room. "Yeah, years ago I dated a kinky guy and he took me. People having sex everywhere. I got totally hot but we just screwed in a room with two other couples, everyone watching everyone. We only touched each other. I know what you need to wear. I'll be back."

She closed the dressing room door behind her. April sat and waited and soon Tammy opened the door and stepped in.

"Two tops. That's it. The other stuff just didn't work. Try these on."

Without hesitation April stripped of her tank top and shorts. She reached behind and released the clasp and her bra popped free. Tammy grinned.

"What? Why are you smiling?"

"No tan lines. You had a hell of a vacation, didn't you?"

"You have no idea."

Tammy held up the first top, a long-sleeved red lace blouse with a high collar, and April moved it aside, taking Tammy's face with both hands and kissing her long and deep. Tammy was stiff for only a half second and then retuned the kiss. They made out silently for a minute and then April rolled the dice. She walked Tammy backward until the salesgirl felt the wall behind her and then April sank to her knees, sliding her hands up under Tammy's short skirt.

"Ohfuckingchrist," Tammy breathed, paralyzed. She covered her mouth with both hands. April folded the girl's skirt up with one hand and pulled her panties to the side with the other. Her head dipped down and under and Tammy felt a hot strong tongue split her pussy. She whimpered through her fingers.

The pretty Asian had a thin pelt of black pubic hair and April sucked the girl's entire vulva into her mouth, twirling her labia with her tongue. The salesgirl's legs trembled and April dove in.

They did their best to be quiet. Tammy came fast and held April's head for support as her hips rocked. Too much time had passed for Tammy to return the favor so April just kissed her cheek and said she'd take the red lace top.

On the walk to the register Tammy, still shaken but the suddenness of April's attack, half turned and said: "You have got to tell me what happened on that goddamn vacation."

April laughed.

Her path out of the mall took her by Pouty and she glanced inside to see if Tony was working. A salesgirl with neon pink hair stood behind the sales counter so April entered.

"Is Tony working tonight?"

Pink Hair looked her up and down with deliberate slowness, her answer snide.

"Nope."

"Thanks." *Who needs this shit?* April spun on a heel and headed for her car.

At home, she tried the top with a multiple of skirts and finally decided on the black pencil. She tried it with a black bra underneath and then with no bra at all.

No bra.

She matched shoes and stood back a few feet from the mirror to see her handiwork. The red lace collar came to just under her chin. Long sleeved and form-fitting, the material flowed around the curves of her heavy breasts and tone arms and back. In the right lighting, she saw the barest hint of a six-pack. The lace was tightly woven so her nipples were not obvious unless she stood straight and pulled her shoulders back. The black pencil skirt made her firm ass look fantastic and she gave herself a smack on the butt.

The doorbell rang. In the living room, she peered through the spyglass and saw Gary on the porch. She looked down.

He'd see plenty.

She opened the door, saying: "You missed Keith. He took the car for a wash and oil change."

Gary couldn't reply for several moments. Once he could, he extended a stack of music CDs. "I borrowed these and I've burned them. Tell Keith thank you. Your outfit looks incredible, April, but where can you wear it?"

"Glad you think so. Keith and I are going to Diablo's this Saturday night. We've heard stories and want to see for ourselves."

"Wow. Just…wow."

She turned left and then right and then pinched the hem and made a small curtsy. She took the CDs. "I'll make sure he gets these. You want something? A bottle of water or something?"

"Yes, please."

He followed April to the kitchen and watched her ass. Once there he took an angle to the refrigerator so when she opened the door the light sliced through the lace.

God fucking damn. I can even see the difference between pink nipple and red lace. Fuck.

She handed him the water and they chatted about business at Gary's three auto repair shops. She was perfectly casual but caught him staring often and enjoyed it very much. At the first uncomfortable silence, Gary excused himself and left. April returned to the bathroom mirror to see what Gary saw.

Diablo sits on the city outskirts, a pariah too far over the line even for Vegas. One street light illuminates the turn-off and the long gravel road to the club is dark.

Gary arrived early and parked well down the street, watching.

Zoned residential, the club had survived dozens of attempts to close it, all failed because it was a private residence. As neighbors moved away, Diablo's bought their homes and turned them into parking lots or added them to the square footage of the original house.

Gary took his cell and wallet and locked his car. His feet crunched pebbles to the front door where a man about sixty asked if this was Gary's first visit. He admitted it was.

"A few rules," the kindly man said. "Behind me is the anteroom. We don't charge to get in but if you'd like to donate, that would be much appreciated. Stella will give you your personal mask. If you leave the anteroom to enter my home, wear it always. We guarantee privacy to everyone."

The old man looked him up and down. "Second rule; the men are naked, every man, all the time. If that makes you too uncomfortable then this is not the club for you. Every other club in Vegas will leave the men clothed and the ladies naked but that's not how we do things here. A woman can disrobe if she wishes but the men must. Understand the rules so far?"

"Yes, sir."

"Okay. The last few are pretty obvious; no pictures, no video, and if someone says no it means no. Keep in mind this is a home I share with my wife. This is not a business. Behave like a guest, not a customer. Don't be that guy. I have big friends who will toss you out naked on the street. It's happened."

"Fair enough. I'm waiting for some friends so I'm going to stand outside. I'll be back soon."

The old-timer gave Gary a nod.

Outside, Gary paced. He knew Keith and April would be angry and hurt if they found out he came to spy on them, but he had to see April wearing that lace top again. When she'd mentioned Diablo's he'd almost choked. Keith and April were his most innocent friends. He knew they'd taken each other's virginity because Keith had bragged about it. What were they doing coming to a place like this? April said they just wanted to look around and Gary totally believed her, but why were they even curious?

Gary found a spot behind a cypress tree that shielded him from view but allowed him to see the street. The parking lot was around the side of the house so when Gary saw them pull in, he'd step inside, strip, get his mask, make his donation, and mingle. The next people through the door would almost certainly be Keith and April. He'd make a note of which masks they wore and then spy on them the rest of the night.

I'm a terrible, terrible best friend. Keith can never know.

Forty-four people arrived before the happy couple. Gary had almost given up, assuming they'd changed their minds. His heart jumped when he saw their car. He zipped inside and handed over his clothing and donned his peacock mask and then passed through the anteroom into the house.

The first area was a family room, wide open with three widescreen television sets and four couches, along with a scattering of plush chairs. A bar ran along the back wall and multiple arches and doorways led further into the sprawling home. Around twenty people sat and conversed or watched TV, all the men nude. Most were over forty with a few younger and a few older.

One couple looked barely eighteen and Gary watched them closely. Within minutes he knew this trip was the girl's idea. She watched everyone but especially loved looking at penises. Size did not matter to her. A man in his mid-thirties started talking to them and soon the girl turned to her boyfriend and said a few words and the boy knelt and began sucking the older man's dick. The girl rested a hand on his head as she returned to chatting with the older man. Soon the three left, moving deeper into the house. A couple older guys followed and Gary guessed that young man would suck them all before they fucked his girl.

Wild.

Gary angled for the bar to watch one of the televisions, porn, with one eye on the front door. He ordered a White Russian. He knew Keith and April might sit in the car for a while or even change their minds so he took his drink and got comfortable behind a pillar. Two women approached and said hello and he was cordial but aloof and they soon departed.

When his friends came through the door he realized how foolish he'd been about the masks. April's body was unmistakable. She wore the same red lace top but this black skirt was much shorter, barely covering her ass. Keith, naked and clearly uncomfortable, wore a black Zorro mask studded with sequins. She wore a small mask of white dove feathers circling her eyes and looking at her made his heart ache.

He pretended to watch the porn and took a slow drink, timing the tumbler in front of his face as they walked across the room and took the first archway. He waited as patiently as he could, which wasn't long, and casually followed, acting as if he were just checking out the club.

The hallway beyond was dark and Gary bumped a birdbath filled with condoms. Three steps down and then another long hallway to the right with open doorways spaced alternating along the length. He strolled, just looking, and on the left passed a wood-panel room with a huge bed in the center and one small red light overhead. A woman straddled a man and fucked him while another man fucked her ass and another, standing, fucked her mouth. The sight shocked him. Out in the open and displaying no guilt whatsoever, the foursome moved with a steady rhythm, punctuated by low moans and groans.

Immediately on the heels of his shock was concern for what his friends would think. He slowed, expecting to find them in the next room on his right, distraught, April in tears and ready to go home. A large leather swing hung from the ceiling, empty, and a bench ran around all four walls. He moved on to the last room.

As he drew near, the faint illumination showed him the hallway did not end but rather a black velvet curtain hung at the end. He peeked into the room and found all four walls mirrored and the ceiling too. A round bed sat in the center and three women and three men enjoyed each other, watched by a half dozen men. He kept going, carefully pulling the heavy black curtain aside. Two feet ahead was a sliding glass door painted black. He heard music faintly, a heavy bass and percussion rhythm. All around the edges of the door multi-colored lights blinked. He slid the door open and stepped through.

This room was big, as big as the family room, but painted black. In the center was a small raised circular stage set with a pole that went up to the ceiling. Flashing and spinning lights gave the space motion and several fog machines kept it filled with mist. His eyes went to the pole because April danced there.

They'd entered a bar area from the rear so he crossed quickly and ordered another drink. Three arches led from this room. Tables surrounded by four chairs each filled the space. A dozen people, including Keith, sat mesmerized as April twirled and spun. She was no expert but she had natural rhythm and enjoyed the attention. Gary paid for his drink and moved to a dark corner to watch.

Her skirt had ridden up and Gary assumed she wore flesh colored panties. A moment later she lifted a leg and he realized he stared at her bare-naked slit. April's open pussy gaped right at him and he groaned, quickly raising his drink to his lips.

Fuck! I can almost see up inside her!

His eyes devoured her. Her big tits swayed and her strong ass, now fully revealed to the crowd, flexed and coiled. He tugged his penis and turned his hips but then realized he had nothing to worry about. All eyes were on April.

A middle-aged woman left her seat and approached the stage, holding some currency out for April. April giggled when she saw it and stopping moving to quietly speak to the woman. She took the money and gave the woman a kiss on the cheek. April returned to dancing and the woman returned to her table with her husband.

Minutes later a short, bald, and heavy man left his seat and moved to the stage, also carrying money in an outstretched hand. Gary smiled until he noticed the man's bouncing penis.

I guess that makes up for being short, bald, and fat.

Gary watched April to see how she took the money but when she saw the penis she stopped and smiled broadly. She turned to Keith and as if transformed into a human elevator, slowly sank to her knees until her face was level with the man's cock and balls. Keith abruptly scooted his chair two steps closer.

Gary had noticed nothing remarkable about Keith's penis when he first entered the club, other than his anxiety seemed to make him shrink some, but now Keith began to grow.

He likes that big cock in April's face?

April opened her mouth and moved it close to the man's member. Gary held his breath. She avoided contact, barely, and the old guy stayed frozen lest he break the spell. April moved her mouth, less than an inch away now, up and down the man's shaft, all while maintaining her gaze with Keith.

Keith had risen to half-staff but paradoxically slowly shook his head. April toyed with the fat man. She opened her mouth wide and moved directly under his hanging shaft, acting as if she was going to engulf the head. She leaned way back and cupped both tits, roughly pinching and pulling her nipples, and then opened her knees, aiming her pussy right at his face. That got a grunt and a small rise out the old guy but had a profound effect on Keith. He tried to hide his erection with his hands, and, failing, moved his chair back and sat, hands on lap.

I'll be damned, Gary thought. *My buddy Keith gets off watching April act slutty. Apparently, she's not allowed to touch though. Too bad.*

Back at the old guy's table his wife clapped and cheered.

April leaned all the way back and lifted her legs off the stage, unfurling and opening them wide. The old man practically drooled.

After teasing the man for a while, April went back to dancing and the fat man returned to his table. His wife gave him a hug. Gary considered offering money too but worried April would see through his disguise. That would be disastrous.

A few songs later April was ready to move on. Keith was soft again and as he stood, Gary compared, pleased he was significant larger than Keith. The happy couple exited through an arch. Gary waited and then followed.

In the next room, a harem theme with two large fountains, Gary realized three other men followed April just like he did. He'd spotted them earlier and thought nothing of it but at last his brain connected the dots.

Can't say I blame them but keep your distance, fuckers.

Keith and April sat on a loveseat and soon started making out. This area had mostly couples in it so Gary had to sit farther away than he wanted to remain discrete. After a while Keith lifted April's top off and played with her tits while they kissed, and not long after that April lowered her head to his lap and started sucking his penis. Gary could not believe his great luck. Watching April suck dick was thrilling all the way down to his toes. Her short skirt rode higher, exposing her pussy, and he got hard and stroked as he watched.

April looked around the room and smiled. All about, couples and single men masturbated watching her and Keith. The men ranged in size, mostly average or smaller, but two of them were nicely long and plump. She put her mouth back on Keith.

Gary was hard as stone. April sucked cock way better than he expected from one so inexperienced. He heard April tell Keith to cum if he could and Keith said he needed a bathroom break first. April leaned back and Keith left.

Gary saw an opportunity and took it. He left his chair and walked towards April, stroking his cock as he went. He hoped his hard dick was distraction enough and it was. April looked him in the eyes and Gary's heart thudded in his chest but the moment passed. She did not recognize him. Her eyes fell to his dick. She'd looked directly at him and he'd escaped detection. He stopped a foot away from her face and jacked his meat. April gazed at his cock with longing and that almost put Gary over the edge. He stared at her naked tits and her naked pussy and her beautiful face and almost shot again.

April stared at his erection and started rubbing her clit.

"Keep an eye out for my husband," she said. "I can't get caught."

She wrapped her free hand around Gary's hot shaft and pumped him. Gary thought he would die. He watched her sweet hand jack up and down and became aware of how hairy he was.

"You're big," she offered.

He pitched his voice deeper. "Lucky me. Biggest you've had?"

He knew he was before he asked the question. He wanted the thrill of hearing her admit it.

"No," she giggled, surprising him. "But one of my top three."

A hundred questions raced through his head but one thought crystalized; *Their vacation. Where did they go and what did they do?*

"You're a Goddess. I want to fuck you."

"That's hot, thank you, but I can't. I promised my husband I wouldn't anymore. God, your cock is nice though. So thick. And you have the hardest dick I've ever felt."

That's because I've wanted you for years! He wanted to shout.

Movement across the room drew his eyes and he saw Keith returning.

"Your husband," he muttered and backed away, returning to his chair. April bit her bottom lip and looked at Gary's cock with regret and loss and Gary was happier at that moment than he could ever remember being.

She fucking wants me. She craves my cock. Oh, God, April wants to fuck me as much as I want to fuck her.

Keith sat and April began sucking him again but this time she frequently looked at Gary. He saw in her eyes she had no idea who he was, nobody is that good an actress, she just wanted to tease him because she wanted to fuck him. His balls felt hot. He had to move or risk cumming. He wanted to stay but April looking at him like that while blowing Keith was too much. He wandered away, erection waving side to side, farther back into the harem room.

At the back was an iron gate and two massive bouncers.

"You must be the guys that throw people into the street naked. What's back there? Management offices?"

"Couples only area. No singles, guys or girls."

"Cool. Thanks."

Gary veered off to circle the rest of the club. Everywhere he went naked people enjoyed each other, singly or as groups. He'd lived in Vegas for decades and never visited this place.

What did she mean, 'I promised my husband I wouldn't anymore?' And I'm in her top three? That must mean she fucked other guys while on vacation.

His erection started to return so he aimed for a bar to hide it, leaning and drinking a fresh white Russian. When he'd calmed down enough, he wandered back to the harem room.

April was on her knees between Keith's legs, bobbing her head like a pigeon. Her hands were clasped behind her back as she tried to make her husband climax using only her mouth and succeeded a moment later. Gary watched April sucking down the salty load, his erection returning yet again.

Oh, for Christ's sake! You're going to kill me, woman.

Keith held her head down and shot her mouth full and sweet, innocent April swallowed like a slut. Gary had to look away. When he looked again, Keith sat with his head hanging off the back of the loveseat and April snuggled him, big tits mashing out under her arms, and softly raked her nails over her husband's sensitive scrotum.

You lucky motherfucker.

They stayed like that until Keith slowly returned to Earth. They chatted quietly until Keith stood.

"I'll be back," he murmured. "I want to wash up and get us fresh drinks."

"Okay, Honey."

They kissed sweetly and Keith walked away.

Gary's legs were moving before he knew he had the thought. He took April's hand and gave it a tug. "Come with me," he said.

She hesitated, frightened. "No."

He leaned down and kissed her mouth, hot and wet. "We have little time, Pretty Dove, take a chance."

April brought a hand up to touch her feathered mask. Gary took the hand and placed it on his hot and hard cock. For some reason, she did not fear this stranger. His voice was strangely reassuring.

"Come with me."

"My husband?"

"We can hide for a short time. I found a place. You can sneak out and rejoin him…after."

April chewed her bottom lip, glancing around at the others. They were busy with each other, inspired by her sucking dick. With his free hand, he held his erection at the base and displayed it proudly. "Look what you've done to me."

"I can't. I want to very much, I swear, but I mustn't." Conflicting emotions twisted her pretty face.

He stepped closer and nudged her lips with his dick. "Open your mouth," he ordered. April obeyed, surprising herself. He pushed his cock in and she wrapped her lips around the head, sucking gently. He did not allow himself time to enjoy the moment. He let her hold his dick in her mouth for only a second and then tugged her hand again.

"Come with me. I promise we have time. You won't get caught."

Almost as if he controlled her mind, April stood.

Gary pulled her along behind him as he headed for the couple's area, talking fast: "Your husband can't come back here without you. We're safe. When you leave go sit someplace out of the way and wait. Just tell him you wanted to prowl the club alone for a minute and you've been waiting there for him the whole time."

They turned a corner and Gary saw the bouncers. He waved for them to open the gate and they did. April and Gary sailed through.

"I can't do this," April protested, once they were beyond the guards.

They entered a series of narrow hallways with small rooms spaced evenly. The doorways were open and the first three taken. On the fourth, Gary pulled her close.

"I must have you, Pretty Dove. Even if only for a moment. I need to feel you wrapped around me. That will be alright, won't it? Just for a second? You want to know how we feel together as much as me."

He kissed her passionately before she could answer.

April felt the electric charge of his years of desire but of course did not fully understand it. What she did understand was his kiss sent shock waves racing through her. She loved feeling desired and somehow this man packed more want behind his kisses than she had defenses for. She felt her will start to crumble.

"But, I promised," she said meekly.

"Blame me," he growled, pulling her body against his, his cock now so hard he jabbed her stomach.

She gripped his cock and squeezed it. Gary saw her forehead wrinkle with need.

"Why are you so hard?"

"You're the most beautiful woman I've ever seen. I've wanted you…from the moment I saw you. I've never reacted like this and please forgive me, I know I'm acting crazy." He kissed her again and felt her melt and impulsively walked her backwards into the small room.

A padded bench hit her behind the knees and she sat, instinctively guiding Gary's cock, now at face level, towards her mouth. He pushed her shoulders back and lifted her legs from behind the knees. Her black skirt around her waist, her red lace top in her other hand, she became the deer in the headlights, allowing his rampant need to dictate what happened to her next.

Gary looked down at her blossoming pussy and leaned forward until his cock head separated her small inner lips. She sucked air in a gasp. The heat from her pussy made his cock swell even harder and he burned the sight and this moment into his mind forever.

Gary drove his cock into April.

She was beyond drenched. He slid in smoothly, enveloped in a blanket of hot and wet. Her tight pussy swaddled him in a lightly sucking furnace and he groaned loudly, as much from the intense pleasure as from the intense knowledge that he was, at long last, buried inside the woman he desired more than any other.

The man's heartfelt groan sent fantastic chills through her. His runaway desire heated her to boiling. She loved hearing the pleasure she gave. She loved feeling so wanted. His cock was fat but the steely rigidity of the organ is what sent shockwaves of pleasure running through her. It felt so good to have a hard, new cock fucking her again. She dropped her lace top as the man began to saw in and out. Stars exploded in her mind. A big cock fucked her again and she was so happy. Maybe it was how bad she was behaving or maybe it was the man's desperate need for her or maybe it was just how hard he was, but the tingling in her pussy started right away.

"I'm...cum," she mewled.

Gary couldn't believe his ears.

"You want to cum, Pretty Dove? Hm? You like my hard dick?"

"Yesssss...."

Gary fucked her harder. His climax threatened from the moment her pussy enfolded him so he pushed it out of his mind. He moved farther over her, covering her with his body. At last he was looking down on beautiful April as he fucked her. With every strong thrust he tried to convey his adoration, lust, and years of unrequited want.

She did feel it. Something about this stranger affected her. She found herself wanting to accept his passion and return it. Although rough, she felt the tender desire behind his touch. Only his passion for her made him rough. She sensed he cared well beyond sex. Her pussy gripped him like a fist and she crossed her ankles behind his head.

"Fuck me," she hissed, giving in completely and pulling his mouth down for another kiss. "Make me cum."

The tingling spread from her clit outward, gathering every muscle and sinew, moving through her hips and back, down her legs and out into her arms. Her pussy tighten around him again.

"Oh, do it, Baby. Fuck me hard. Let me cum for you. Make me cum on your hard cock. Christ! Almost! Yeah! Ooooohhhhhh fuck, yesssssss!"

Gary could not believe it. April Willet loved his cock. April was cumming on his cock. His! He bumped his efforts up another level and she wailed her pleasure as she climaxed. Her sounds in his ear were too much. Her tight pussy milking his rod was too much. His hot bouncing balls were too much, and he thundered and released a flood of sperm, spraying wildly inside her, coating every inch of her walls and womb. He thought his orgasm would never end. His body jerked and convulsed and a stream of cum blasted from him. He rolled his head and arched his back and pumped every drop he had inside sweet, sweet April.

When he finished, he pulled his hard cock from her body like withdrawing a sword. He stood frozen between her trembling legs. His cock refused to go soft. April absentmindedly ran her hands over her sensitive skin and looked down her body at his defiant erection.

"I like that," she murmured, pointing. "You want me again?"

"And again and again and again."

She smiled. "I'm your Pretty Dove and you're my Sexy Peacock." She dabbed a finger at her opening. "That's a lot of cum."

Impulsively, he considered revealing himself to her and explaining everything. He smothered the idea.

"I had a lot of want," he said.

She indicated his hard dick with a jerk of her chin. "Still do."

"Yes. Very much. More than you know."

Some quality in his voice melted her. She heard real want, not mere lust. She sat and then stood. A fog seemed to clear from her mind.

"Hand me my top, please. We need to go."

She tugged her skirt down. Gary handed her the red lace top. He wanted to say something meaningful but nothing came to him.

Dressed again, April motioned towards the door. Gary led the way.

Just before they passed through the gate, she kissed him again. "I want to fuck you again. I'll try to get my husband to come back in two weeks. Saturday night, around ten. I hope to see you."

"I'll be here."

She kissed him again. "My Sexy Peacock."

"My Pretty Dove."

Gary exited first and scanned for Keith and then waved her out. She circled well away from the bathrooms and found a spot in the room with the pole dancing, buying a drink and sitting behind a pillar. She got an idea and tapped out a message to Keith but then dimmed her phone without sending it.

I might be a little too good at this.

Frustrated, that's where Keith found her. He sat her wine on the table. "I've been searching for ten minutes, April. Why did you leave?"

"I'm so sorry, Honey. I sent you a text. See?"

She went through the charade of checking her phone.

"Damnit. I never hit send. I'm sorry, Baby. I wandered the club a little and then sat here watching the girls dance. I wondered what happened to you."

Keith kissed the top of her head. They sat a long time and then meandered more of the club. April saw Peacock tailing them several times. She liked that he didn't just get his rocks off and leave.

At the back of the house they found a spiral staircase down which led to a game room with billiards and foosball. The room had at least a dozen men in it. On the far side was a door with the word "Glorious" painted above it.

Keith opened the door and ushered April through and then closed the door behind them. They followed a long hallway which opened into a rounded area with a circular booth in the center perhaps five feet across. All around the booth, holes had been cut in the walls around waist height. The door to the booth was open so Keith stepped in and April followed. They were cramped in the tiny space. He shut the door and the outside lights went dark.

Inside the booth the circular walls were covered with hardcore erotic and pornographic posters of various sex-acts. In the center of the small room was a stool. Keith sat but April slowly surveyed each poster, studying the graphic sex.

When the first penis came through the wall she did not see it. Keith did and mentioned it and she looked where he pointed and then back at him.

"What the hell?" she asked.

From different holes a second and third penis emerged. April looked through an empty hole but the outside was too dark to see anything. She stepped back to Keith.

Three more penises appeared. They were all varying sizes, shapes, and colors but she thought none was particularly large or pretty. She laughed once and started to sit on Keith's knee but at the last moment remembered her cum-filled pussy. Worried she'd soak his pants, she remained standing.

A seventh penis came through the wall, a large black one, and she faced her husband expectantly.

"You want to play with that one?" he asked.

"Can I suck it?" She looked around the small room. "You don't have to worry about me fucking anyone in here," she joked, nervously. "No room."

He studied her face for a moment. "Alright." He kissed her and left.

April took his seat and leaned for the black cock. It was covered with squiggly veins and had a large flared head. She lifted it to feel the weight and was surprised by the heat. She pulled the loose skin, drawing more of the shaft into the room with her, and then worked his balls over the padded edge. She leaned back to appreciate it; a nice long, fat, black cock hung down her wall. She giggled and leaned farther back. Seven dicks hung in front of her, all different sizes, all different levels of firmness.

It looks like an art gallery at Marquis De Sade's place.

She leaned forward and opened her mouth. The black cock smelled like cologne and tasted faintly of shampoo. She slid it into her mouth and was rewarded by a deep groan through the wall.

The area took on a buzz of excitement. She started sucking, feeling him grow in her mouth, and reached for others. Her hands stayed busy moving from penis to penis but her mouth stayed with the black. When Keith's penis dropped through a hole, she kissed the head but otherwise ignored it.

I'm sure he's just watching me anyway.

One of the dicks she masturbated shot over her hand and withdrew. Moments later an erect cock she recognized slipped through.

My Sexy Peacock has recovered and wants more.

April felt a surge of heat rise in her. This cock had secretly fucked her less than an hour ago and now she would suck it right in front of her husband.

I'm a horrible person, she thought, closing her mouth on the head. *I'm full of a stranger's cum, no longer on birth control, and sucking the same stranger's dick in front of my ignorant man. What level of Hell will be reserved for me?*

She split her attention between the nice black cock and the nice white one. She jerked off a few more but then gave up on them, giving all her love and attention to her two men. She felt Keith's eyes on her and that caused guilt, but she felt far stronger waves of erotic pleasure.

Black grew slowly, filling with blood and slightly curving to the right. White was already hard when it came through the hole and just continued to grow a deeper shade of red. She pinned the white dick to the wall and slobbered his big balls with her tongue. The scent of her pussy on his cock made her clit tingle.

Soon both slabs of beef gleamed with her saliva. Keith still hung limp but April wasn't surprised; she'd swallowed him so recently he'd need time to recover. Until then, she was free to play. She told herself not to back her ass to the wall and fuck either of these men but the idea of taking her first black cock set her mind spinning.

There's something extra exciting about a black dick. Like I'm being an especially bad wife.

She channeled her lust into her blowjobs and sucked hard, jerking the men with enthusiasm. Black started to leak cum and she held the shaft up at the base and squeezed. A pearl appeared on top. She found the hole with Keith's watchful eyes and licked the sperm away while gazing at her husband. She heard him mutter, "Jesus Christ," and she giggled.

She moved both hands to Black and stroked as she sucked. His deep grunts excited her. She felt his cock swell and sucked harder and he growled a warning but she only sucked harder and faster. He understood and his hips began to bang the wall.

All at once he yelled and April felt a hot blast of cum hit the back of her throat. He was tangy and incredibly salty but she ignored her gag reflex and sucked his cum out. Every time he cried some unintelligible sound and shot another jet into her maw, she smiled on the inside.

I love reducing big strong men to whimpering children.

He tried to pull back but she held him by the shaft and balls on her side of the wall, sucking hard, swirling the crown with her tongue, feeling his legs buckle and hearing his body stumble against the wall. Only when he stopped leaking completely did she release him with a pop. He staggered backward, mumbling.

She turned her attention to Peacock. She'd ignored him for many minutes but he remained hard as ever. She blocked Keith's view with a thigh and dabbed a finger in her flooded pussy again to remind her of the cum this man had deposited there. The act made her feel raunchy and slutty. Peacock wasn't as long as James or as thick as Michael, but he was certainly bigger than her husband, and that thrilled her.

She grabbed the dick with both hands and bent it to her mouth. Carefully pushing him deep, she adjusted her jaw and tongue constantly. She wanted him as far in her mouth as she could get him, partly for herself, partly showing off for her husband. She enjoyed the feeling of a hot, pulsing shaft in her mouth. She took her time, worked him deeper, breathed through her nose and pushed him deeper still. His pubic bone was still several inches away when she realized she'd not be able to take him all. She began to bob with tiny movements of her head.

After the initial rush when he almost blew his load too fast, Gary calmed down and made April work his cock. A hole in the wall down and to his left allowed him to catch occasional glimpses of her pretty face and his dick in her mouth, and he was prepared to remain standing at that wall the rest of his life.

April is sucking my cock. April is sucking my cock! I never thought this possible.

He loved the way she worked him; twirling her tongue, licking his balls, slathering his shaft as she pulled her mouth up the shaft. This had to be Heaven.

He lasted fifteen minutes. The excitement was too much and in the end, she moved back to concentrate on his head and that allowed him to see her face and that put him over the edge. He knew she'd swallowed the black guy's load so he gave her no warning, guessing right that she'd welcome his too. She tortured him too, sucking through his climax and long after, but he welcomed it, growling and groaning as sweet April slutted it up.

When she let go he proudly noted he was still mostly erect.

Keith opened the door. "That was awesome."
"You liked it?"
"Loved it."

April stood and kissed him with her slippery mouth. "Me too. Slutty is better than frightened introvert. Can we come back in a couple weeks?"

"Hell yes."

They returned to the pole-dancing bar and had one last drink. The girl on the pole was chubby but talented and everyone cheered for her. Once the song ended she returned to her friends. April turned to Keith.

"I've been wondering something; was it exciting for you earlier when you couldn't find me? Tell the truth."

"It was."

"Why?"

"Because my imagination ran wild. I envisioned you doing all sorts of naughty things."

"But if it was exciting that means you wanted me to do naughty things. At least a big part of you wanted that. You searched the club hoping you'd find me fucking someone."

"Yes, part of me did. A bigger part hoped you'd honor our agreement."

April made a quizzical face. "What agreement?"

"The one where I asked you not to do anything behind my back because it makes me uneasy."

April laughed. "I remember that conversation ending very differently. We have no agreement. I told you to trust me and you stopped talking."

"Hm."

April rolled her eyes. "I swear men have a gene that makes them need to control women; fathers over daughters, husbands over wives, even brothers over sisters."

"I don't want to control you."

"Bullshit."

"Because I don't want you fucking men behind my back?"

"No. Keith, it's not the fucking them, it's the fucking them behind your back. Think about that. Why do you need to know? It's about controlling me. You're fine with me fucking them, you just need to feel like you've granted permission. Like I'm yours to hand out to other men. It turns you on so you use me for your own pleasure. What about mine? Why do your rules cover me?"

"Then why be married?"

"Weak. Listen, we can create any marriage we want. We don't need to define our marriage in the ways we've been taught. What do we want? That's the marriage we should live. Forget the church and forget your parents; what do *we* want? They aren't in charge of us and from what I've seen of previous generations, I don't want them to be. They can keep their stupid rules for themselves. Do we even know a happily married older couple? Have courage, Keith. Right now, you've got one foot in the canoe and one foot on the shore. Let's get in and paddle."

"So, you get to fuck anyone you want, wherever and whenever you want?"

"That sounds hot."

"That sounds like cheating. Why would you cheat if you know I'll allow it anyway? Why not just get my buy-in first?"

"Oh, for fuck's sake. Flip that around! If you know you're going to allow it, why play the silly game? I know you'll say yes. You know you'll say yes. We both love it too much. Stop looking at this like cheating. You just have a need to keep your wife under control. You're just trying to protect your fragile male ego. Like I belong to you and you're allowing me this freedom and that lets you save face. I'm saying there's no face to save. Forget what others say. Forget what they want you to think. This is ours."

Keith looked down at his hands, quietly thoughtful for long minutes. "I'm starting to understand what you're driving at. I think I get what you're saying. I feel like if I agree I'm giving up control, which matches what you were saying, but I suspect I never really had any control, did I?"

"No, and I'm not suggesting I'm looking to keep secrets. I just want total freedom. I'll always tell you, just not always before. I want to allow for spontaneity."

Keith fretted, rubbing his sweaty palms on his bare legs. "Why does this feel scary?"

April shrugged. "That's a great question you should ask yourself."

Keith looked around the room. Nothing had changed; couples talked, drank, danced, laughed. Nothing had changed but he felt like his world had shifted away from a comfortable place. *This will take some getting used to.*

"So if I say yes, can I fuck other women?"

April regarded her husband with a coy smile. "Sure, Honey, if that what you want. If that's what makes you feel like we're equals. Is that what you want to do?"

Keith scanned the women in the room. His breathing slowed. Even if April said yes, he had to admit that's not what he wanted, not truly. Nothing beat watching April. If he fucked another it would be a lie. For a moment, he felt trapped by his own desires. Then a calm warmth spread through him. *I should just embrace the real me.*

April glanced around the room too but for entirely different reasons. Already feeling her new freedom, April was sizing up the men present. Fortunately for Keith at that moment she found none of the surrounding men attractive.

I wonder where Peacock wandered off to? She pondered. *Although fucking him again after just sneak-fucking and sucking him might be too much. Maybe we should just call it a night.*

April rested a hand on her lower abdomen, just above her pussy, and looked at Keith who watched an older woman work the stripper pole.

Guess I better pick up more Mifepristone, she thought. That she carried another man inside her unprotected womb excited her.

Monday morning back at the bank proved dreadful. At first Keith described their vacation with words like amazing and fantastic but as his colleagues pressed him for details he realized what he could reveal only made the vacation sound utterly average. He talked less about it as the day wore on.

At Pepperdine Manufacturing, when April walked through the front doors Monday morning, work ground to a halt. Beyond her new body and new look, April radiated something that day she'd never possessed before. Her confidence, the certainty of who she was and what she wanted from life, made her glow. Heads turned left and right, male and female. Janet Crum, her best friend at work, wanted to know what happened. April tried to pass her change of as the relaxation of a vacation well spent but Janet wasn't buying it.

"No, this goes far beyond that. You're a changed girl. In fact, it's like you're no longer a girl at all. It's like the time away turned you into a woman."

April beamed. She felt eyes on her all day.

After work she stopped by the gym. She'd eaten poorly and consumed way too much alcohol so hitting the weights and treadmill hurt.

At home that night she and Keith cuddled on the couch to watch a movie and then went to bed. After so much chaos, a well-established routine felt good. Every night that week and the next they hurried to the comfort of their couch, cuddling and snuggling and thoroughly enjoying each other.

On Thursday Gary called Keith and suggested they watch the basketball game together. Keith sent April a text letting her know they'd have company that night.

She remembered they had planned another trip to Diablo's for Saturday night only two days from now and that sent a surge of electricity running around her body. The repetition of everyday life had so quickly enveloped them their vacation adventures had begun to fade.

She text back that she'd need a new outfit for Saturday night so she'd go shopping after work. Keith and Gary could have the place to themselves.

At nine o'clock that night April walked through the front door.

"No one leave," she ordered, headed for the bedroom. *This should be fun.*

When she returned, Keith paused the game. She wore black boots to mid-thigh, a pleated black mini-skirt, and a pink gossamer top with black-lace bra beneath.

"Aright, gentlemen, I need your opinion because I can't decide. Gary, Keith and I are going to a private club on Saturday and I don't know what to wear. This is the first of two outfits. Wait until you see both to tell me your recommendation."

She turned slowly, enjoying the looks of astonishment on each man's face. She'd worn the bra for Keith to avoid embarrassing him in front of his best friend but at the club she'd be braless. She answered their questions about comfort and style and then disappeared into the bedroom, reappearing minutes later in a black floor-length dress with high collar and long sleeves. Simple, but elegant, and the fabric clung to every curve and when the track lights hit her, both men saw faint areola.

"I say outfit one," offered Gary. "You looked stunning, outrageously sexy."

Keith agreed, although the depth of Gary's enthusiasm surprised him a little.

"Thank you, guys. You can return to your game now."

Gary waited until April left the room and Keith looked away. His dick was hard and he pushed it to the side. Keith and April would return to Diablo's as planned.

With a little luck, I'll fuck her again forty-eight hours from now.

He couldn't wait.

April set the bedroom door so a half-inch gap remained. Keith could not see it from his chair but Gary could and he now understood she did these things intentionally. With stolen glances, he watched April slip out of her clothing and cross the bedroom nude several times. He knew she was watching and allowed her to catch him staring.

She loved the way he looked at her. She considered showing him more but held back; this was her husband's best friend and *some* rules should apply. Finally, she pulled on a short robe, loosely tied, and joined the men to watch the last of the game.

Saturday evening, Gary entered his bathroom. Earlier in the day he'd purchased a trimmer and new razor and he set to work. An hour later he had a light smattering of hair on his chest and arms but the rest of his body was neatly trimmed. He turned his hips in the mirror, surprised how much bigger his dick looked.

I should have done this long ago.

He showered and ran the razor all around his cock and balls. The nude organ looked intensely sexual, like cutting the hair away had turned a spotlight on it. He knew April would approve. After, he scrubbed and then sprayed cologne. He dressed in comfortable sweats because the club would make him take them off. He climbed into his car and drove, arriving twenty minutes before the Willets. He'd text Keith earlier on the pretense of coming over to borrow music and Keith had replied he had to get there soon because they were leaving the house at nine.

Gary smiled. "I'll come over Tuesday or Wednesday instead. Have fun!"

Tonight, he entered the club and got comfortable. He knew what April would be wearing so no need to hide and watch. He'd requested the peacock mask and it was available so he wore it now and nothing else. The cool club air on his skin felt stimulating. At nine-fifteen, they walked through the door. April wore the high-boots, short skirt, and gossamer top but she'd skipped the bra and Gary gasped. His cock started to rise. Keith wore a red courtesan mask and April sported a small white porcelain cover with delicate painted lines.

I will never tire of looking at her.

He knew he didn't love her, not in a romantic way. This was no adolescent crush like Keith thought. This was raw lust. From the moment he'd first seen her, he'd wanted her, but to fuck, to ravage, to conquer, not to adore, not to worship from afar.

He followed them around the club as he had last time, waiting for his opportunity. He noticed April glancing around the club often so he placed himself in her line of sight. She looked right through him. When Keith left for the restroom he moved but so did three other men. April looked a little overwhelmed and since the others got to her first he found himself walled off, struggling to say hello over their voices.

Finally, he said: "Pretty Dove?" and April looked past the men surrounding her.

"Peacock? Is that you?" She gently pushed them aside. Gary stepped forward.

Her eyes traveled his slick body and a grin spread across her face. "I didn't recognize you. Did you do that for me?" She waved a finger around his body indicating all he'd shaved.

"I did. Can we slip away?"

"No. Have a seat, Join my husband and me."

Inside, Gary panicked. Keith would not be so distracted by a naked male body. Gary knew he might be discovered and then forced to face the most awkward and uncomfortable scene of his life. He glanced nervously at the restroom. The other men looked at him annoyed.

"Find me later," he blurted, backing away. "Your husband present makes me uncomfortable."

April tilted her head, surprised, but nodded. Gary returned to his barstool. When the bathroom door opened, the men scattered. Keith saw them leaving.

"Fan club?" he asked as he took his seat.

"Yes, in fact," April chuckled.

They talked about the other people there and some of the girl's outfits and then April let slip there was a man there she wanted to fuck. Keith felt his blood turn to cold water.

"Who?"

"He's shy. You make him nervous. He came over and said hello while you were gone and I like him. He's got a fat dick."

Keith drew a deep breath, wondering if he'd ever get used to this life.

"So, what happens now?"

"Is that a yes?"

Keith steadied himself and gave a definitive nod.

April leaned over the table and kissed him.

"Then you wait here and I'll be back later. Let your imagination run wild. I'll want you to fuck my brains out after."

Keith couldn't believe how comfortable his wife had become. She slid from her seat and kissed him again and then crossed the room to talk to a man leaning at the bar. The man was tall and pale-skinned and lean. He wore a mask of peacock feathers. April was right about the fat cock and the man seemed to be growing an erection just from speaking to April. His large organ was hairless and so freshly shaved it gleamed. They continued talking and Keith felt his own penis stir.

April glanced over often to see how her husband was handling this new role and she must have liked what she saw because she took the man's hand and held it. The simple act stabbed Keith's eyes and made him gasp. He moved forward on his chair so his swelling penis hung off the edge. It killed him to watch April with another but he had to admit the excitement was intense.

April stepped closer and scooped the man's hairless scrotum into her palm. Keith sucked air and held it. She hefted the weight and Keith wished he'd gone over the condom rule with her again.

No way she'll forget.

The man jumped at her touch and his penis lifted rapidly until it seemed to strain to reach her. Keith took two big gulps of his whiskey. April rolled the large balls around inside their fleshy sack and then drew her small hand up the shaft. She teased the head with her fingertips, tickling under the tip, and then rolled around a droplet of cum she found at the slit. Keith moaned. Despite himself, he wanted to see his pretty wife suck it.

April squeezed the man firmly around the shaft and pulled him away from the bar. She mashed her big tits against his chest and gazed up into his eyes. Keith wondered why they didn't kiss and then realized the mask most likely prevented it.

Thank Jesus for small favors.

The man took April's hand and led her from the room. Keith stood, half erect, intending to follow but stopped after one step. Several others followed April and her new lover out of the room but Keith held back.

He didn't want me there so I'm sure April doesn't either.

That knowledge hurt even as it inflamed.

Fuck! My wife is going off to fuck another man in private!

He stared at the archway where they had left the room and felt his penis pulse. His appreciation for April's point was growing rapidly; imagination is worse than reality. He knew he'd spend each moment she was away in torturous agony and she'd intuitively understood this. This moment carried an erotic charge like no other.

An older woman walked up to his shoulder and spoke: "She's got you hard as steel. My husband's the same way. I saw the way that man looked at her. He's going to fuck her like a savage."

Keith slowly faced the woman. She smirked and walked away.

Gary led April to the couple's area. The bouncers gave a quick nod and opened the gate. Gary led her farther back this time, all the way back to the last small room. April entered and sat on the padded bed.

"Leave your clothes on," he told her. "You look stunning."

April grinned and opened her clutch. She withdrew a condom and held it towards Gary with two fingers.

He stared at it.

"I'm not on birth control," she said.

"Were you last time?"

"No."

That news sent a rush through Gary. "Then why use one this time?"

"Last time I lost my head. Sneaking away was terribly exciting. Fucking you felt so good. But I shouldn't have done that. I promised my husband."

Gary stepped closer. His big erection bumped her hand. "No."

"Then this isn't happening, Big Boy."

Gary took his cock in hand and slowly began to stroke. "Stand up and turn around slowly. Let me look at you. Make my dick even harder."

April hesitated for an instant and then did as he asked. She loved the way he looked at her. His eyes burned with desire through the slits of his mask and sent shivers through her. She put the condom back in her clutch and set it in the corner. She backed against the padded bed until the edge touched her hamstrings. Gary added his other hand and stroked his large dick using both fists in time.

"I know what you're trying to do and it won't work," she teased.

"What's that?"

"You think you can get me so turned on with your big cock I'll fuck you bare anyway. Don't bother. I won't give in."

"Actually, I just want to look at you and stroke my dick. You're fucking hot. Like the hottest I've ever seen. There's something about you that gets to me and I love looking at you. Open your legs a little."

April scrutinized him checking for bullshit. She opened her legs. He saw she wore tiny black panties and told her to remove them slowly.

April enjoyed this game. His cock had her wet, there was no denying that, but his gaze is what really lit her mind on fire. He made her feel like the most beautiful woman in the world. She stood and slid the panties down her legs and kicked them into the corner by her purse.

"Sit. Open your legs again."

April did as he instructed. His eyes roamed from her legs to her bald pussy, over her fit body to her firm tits. He stopped at her eyes.

"God," he croaked. "You're like a fucking angel."

She pulled her skirt up and began fingering her pussy. His cock was so big and hard. Her mouth watered and her pussy ached with emptiness but she knew she couldn't without protection.

I can suck it though.

She leaned forward. Gary understood instantly and pushed his hips towards her mouth. She sucked the tip and then eased the head farther in. Gary sighed. Looking down at April Willet sucking his cock was a dream come true. He rested a hand on each of her shoulders just to feel her body move as she pleased him.

After a few minutes, he said he needed to sit and they traded places. Gary propped his back against the wall with his legs out in front of him and April climbed on the bed between them. She got her mouth on his cock again, her ass high in the air and pointed towards the door. Each person that walked by saw a perfect view of her dripping slit bracketed by her high black boots.

He let her suck to her heart's content. She commented more than once about how hard he got and how much she loved that so he just leaned back and let her please him. When a single black man stopped at the doorway to watch, Gary gave him a wicked grin. The man was older and his chest covered lightly with salt-and-pepper short curly hair. His cock was uncircumcised and big, hanging down as he watched April suck. He masturbated, eyeing April like she was a slab of meat, and his penis began to fill. Soon he was hard and jacking off watching April suck.

Gary got an idea.

He took April's wrists in each hand and pulled her arms under his legs so she rested on her elbows.

"Just use your mouth," he told her.

She eagerly complied. He leaned forward slightly to pin her arms with his weight and then reached back and grabbed her ass cheeks in each hand, lewdly spreading them. The older black man smiled. April's cunt lay wide open before his probing gaze. He moved closer. April was utterly unaware of his existence.

"Take all of my cock," Gary ordered.

April loved the way he told her what to do. She drew a deep breath and then eased his meat to the back of her mouth. She felt him place a hand on the back of her head, nudging her forward, encouraging her to take more. She pushed her throat down and felt his head slip over her tongue and bump her tonsils. Pride filled her. She controlled her gag reflex well.

Pressure split her labia. For a moment, she was confused, thinking Peacock must have thick fingers, but then realized he still held both ass cheeks open.

A huge and hot tube of meat worked deeper.

"Nuuu gghhhung!" she cried around the cock in her throat. "Nuung! Sthhhapgit!

She tried to crawl forward away from the cock she now knew was penetrating her an inch at a time but Gary's hard dick stopped her. His hand on the back of her head kept her from pulling her mouth off and his weight on her arms kept her pinned. The cock pushed another inch deep and she saw stars. It felt astonishing. She moaned before she could stop herself and tried to struggle again but hands came down on her hips and that fat cock drove three more inches deep. All the air left her lungs.

"Unnnngh! Ohfgingud!"

Gary held her in place as the man behind her pushed the rest of his dick in. Despite her dire situation, the sensation that shoved its way to the forefront of her mind was the knowledge she had two cocks inside her at the same time. The reality was a splinter in her brain. She felt like a spit-roast. She imagined what she must look like and a mini orgasm shook her hips.

Gary felt her cum. "Oooooh, sweet Baby. You like this. Okay, we'll give it to you then. Help me fuck her, bro."

The cock in her pussy began sawing in and out. He felt huge and she arched her back in pleasure each time he thrust forward. The two men matched rhythm quickly and April felt herself receiving cock from both ends and loved it. Soon the balls behind her began slapping her clit and she knew the stranger had his entire length in her. She sucked hard and Gary groaned.

"Bitch loves it," the man behind her said.

April tried to pushed her hips back at him in time with his thrusts. His cock was a spear inside her, opening her up, stretching her small tunnel, penetrating the depths of her. She felt another orgasm start to build.

Two cocks! I'm getting fucked at both ends. Two men at the same time!

It thrilled her Keith was not there to see it.

Fuck! Here it cums!

She grunted and moaned around Gary's dick and both men understood. Gary pulled her down onto his cock and held her body steady. The man behind her began to hammer her little pussy and she saw herself again and her brain exploded. She screamed around the cock in her mouth. Her pussy gushed fluid, dripping and splashing around the hard piston in her cunt. She came hard, trapped between them, writhing in what little space she had.

"Oh, hell yeah," the gravel voice behind her muttered. Still rolling on waves of orgasmic pleasure she was only dimly aware the man behind her was jerking with spasms as his cock spit a huge load into her womb. He came a long time and April rode the euphoria with him. At last she felt him slow and then soften and he smacked her ass and he pulled his shank from her inseminated guts.

Gary and the man bumped fists and the man left. When Gary rolled April onto her back she offered no protest. She felt him crawl between her legs so she spread them and looked down her body at his magnificent erection. She reached to guide him in.

Gary expected a pussy full of semen. He expected a cream filled tunnel but the man must have shot so deep none had trickled out yet. He began to fuck April slow and deep. She wrapped her legs around his waist. Her earthshaking climax had her feeling dreamy and she pulled his mouth down to kiss. After the kiss, she pushed her mask off.

"You are so fucking beautiful," he breathed. Now he had April beneath him in all her glory. His cock surged even harder and April moaned. She reached for his mask.

"You don't want to do that," he cautioned.

"I don't care if you're unattractive. I think you're gorgeous. I love the way you look at me and I want to see your face."

Gary held his breath but kept his hips moving in and out. He gave a nod.

April slid his mask up and off. Confusion cast a shadow over her face for a second, then another. Then understanding poured in. Her eyes grew big. Her mouth opened and a hand came up to cover it.

"Gary," she whispered.

"Yes."

She was frozen. Her mind raced in so many directions she remained in one spot. Gary wisely kept his hips moving in a slow and steady rhythm and that's what anchored her and brought her back to the moment. She pulled his head down for another kiss.

"Did you know that man?"

"No," Gary replied.

April whimpered. "A stranger fucked me?"

"Yes."

Her eyelids fluttered. April slid her hands down Gary's body to his ass and felt the rising and falling of his pelvis. "I love the way you fuck, Gary. I love your cock."

"Not the biggest you've had though, right?"

"No."

"I thought Keith took your virginity."

"He did. I fucked men while on vacation."

Gary watched her face and knew she was telling him only the truth.

"I want to cum inside you," he said.

"I want that too."

She snaked her legs around his and kissed him deeply. Gary began fucking April with strokes the length of his cock. Each time his balls rested on her asshole, he'd pressed forward, driving another inch deep. Soon he had April moaning and groaning. He began to drive his hips faster and she told him she could cum again.

"Would you like that, Gary? You want me to cum all over your hard cock? Will we keep our hands to ourselves when you come visit after this?"

Gary moved faster.

"UUunnngh, that's good, Baby. Fuck me. Drive that big cock into me. I love it. I can feel how much you want me, Baby. Fuck me like you're stealing me from Keith. Fuck me like a whore."

Gary raised his body on his arms and started hammering her.

"Here it comes, Gary. Make me cum. Here it comes. Here it is. Ooooooh yeahhhhh!"

Gary felt April clench all around him and milk his shaft. The sensation was too much and pushed him over the edge and he began to spurt his load inside her. She hugged him fiercely, driving her hips at him and urging him to give every drop. When he'd shot his last, he rolled off her.

After a long silence, April spoke: "Don't tell Keith. Put your mask back on before we leave. I'll tell him when the time is right. Did you come to this place two weeks ago because I told you we were or was our meeting pure chance?"

"I came here looking for you."

"You're a shitty best friend."

Gary laughed. "I am, there's no way around that. I was a great best friend until it came down to a choice between that friendship and you. Any other choice and I would have stuck with Keith."

She grinned. "I'm a shitty wife. This vacation opened a door I didn't know existed. No way was I going back. Keith and I will work things out and find an equilibrium but for now I'm kind of running wild. He only hates it a little. Part of him loves it. We're still figuring everything out. Who fucked me from behind?"

"Some older black guy with a long uncircumcised cock."

April's eyes bugged out. "Shut the fuck up! Seriously?"

"Yup. You made him very happy. Lucky fucker."

As usual, she dabbed a finger into her sperm filled pussy. "My first black man and I never even saw his face. That's slutty and decadent."

"He was handsome in a way. If older men are okay."

"Absolutely. I bet I can find him out in the club. I'll look. Describe him to me. I need to get back to Keith."

They lay a few more minutes as Gary told her everything he could remember about the man. They replaced their masks and left separately.

Keith sat where April had left him, a hard penis poking up from his lap. April felt like she'd been gone forever and was surprised to learn it was only forty-five minutes or so. Keith tried to play it cool but the dam burst and he peppered her with a million questions. She told him exactly what happened minus Gary's identity.

"They came inside you? Both?"

"Yes. Honey, I get too excited. I lose track of everything except that hard cock fucking me. I'm a very bad girl."

"Take me back to the couple's area. Show me the room where they fucked you. It's my turn and I won't be gentle."

April's eyes flared. "I like that. Reclaim your slut, Honey."

Keith did. He was rougher than he'd ever been but April just seemed to welcome it. Even when he worried he'd crossed a line she just moaned and urged him on. He added his cum to theirs and they slept like babies that night.

At work all the next week, Keith was pensive. Conflict devoured him. He understood everything April said and her position carried a lot of logic, but he could not divest himself emotionally. What she wanted felt wrong to him. Every time she sent a text or called, he jumped, sure she was going to tell him she'd spent the day fucking another man and was now leaving Keith for a bigger bank account and bigger dick.

She's right, I do feel a sense of ownership, but I feel it all the way down to my DNA. There are probably evolutionary reasons and I can't overcome them. I need someone to talk to but who can I share something this bizarre with?

Half an hour later his phone buzzed. Gary sent a text asking if Keith wanted to hang out and watch the game after work.

Gary is my best friend. I can tell him anything. It will be awkward at first but he doesn't judge. I'll tell him to come over and then when the moment is right, tell him I need to talk.

April Willet pushed back from her cluttered desk. Work had been a monster since her return with no end in sight.

Nobody had stepped in to do her work while she was away, they just left it for her when she returned.

She minimized her window and opened the news just to distract herself. She skimmed world events and zoomed in on US stories. Three pages down, A headline glared back at her, the story below.

> VOODOO MUSEUM BUSTED;
> New Orleans.
> Police today arrested Dancier LePerg, alleged leader of an underground Satanic sex cult operating out of the Voodoo museum in New Orleans. An FBI spokeswoman had announced the discovery of a hidden church, complete with hallucination inducing candles and powerful aphrodisiac lotions and oils. Police were alerted to the scene when two customers, husband and wife, stumbled across a secret shrine. The wife inadvertently contacted the oils.
> "My wife was a totally different woman after that," said Vincent Grum, husband. "She found a statue with, um, exaggerated male characteristics and the oil spurt on her hands. After that, she was a sex-fiend for months."
> Cops say unsuspecting tourists were lured into committing bizarre sex-acts with parishioners as part of subversive rituals designed to indoctrinate them into the cult.

The picture showed the withered black man from behind the counter. There was more to the story but April had read enough. She remembered the obscene statue with the enormous cock.

I stroked that statue and I bet that wife did too. That milky fluid Keith found on my T-shirt must have been drug laced. I touched and smelled it. I even tasted it.

Her mind skipped back and then worked forward.

Right after that I met David and sucked his cock within hours. Oh, my God.

The longer she thought about it, the more she recalled an insidious presence lurking in her veins at every carnal decision.

How many times did those aphrodisiacs affect me? How much of what I did was purely my own choice or at the subtle manipulations of mind-altering drugs? And speaking of drugs, how did the ecstasy affect it? I went wild that night! Would I have otherwise? I thought I was being bold and my true self. What if I was just a mind-controlled puppet?

She went back over every sex decision she'd made the last few weeks. A growing sense of dread filled her heart.

I must tell Keith about this.

As she reached for her phone it chimed with a message from her husband; "Gary is here, hanging out. What time you home tonight?"

Her world caved in.

Fuck! Gary! I slept with my husband's best friend!

Her hands came up and held her face. The news had shifted her perspective and she saw herself as an outsider would see her.

What the fuck was I thinking? I did *cheat on him. My rationalizations are pure bullshit. I should never need to hide anything.*

With trembling fingers, she text back: "Gym after work, home around 8:30-9:00"

Nervous fingers of ice crept up her legs.

I'm so stupid. I've risked everything. I'll confess and show Keith this article and blame everything I did on the drugs in that ejaculate I tasted. It will be like hitting a reset button with him. I'll promise to never again do anything he disapproves and only do what he wants. Fuck, I hope I didn't mess this marriage up.

Time ticked off slowly. At the end of her work day April no longer felt like visiting the gym and drove straight home. She pulled into the garage and dropped her purse in the kitchen. She drew a deep breath, telling herself to be patient.

No way can I bring this up in front of Gary.

The men sat in the living room. A basketball game was on the television but the sounds was off. Both men had several empty beer bottles in front of them.

"Hi, Honey," she chirped, kissing Keith. "How are you, Gary?"

"I'm great, thanks. Just hanging out with my best buddy, Keith."

Their voices sound strained and awkward to April but Keith said nothing. He patted the open spot next to him on the couch.

"Have a seat, baby. I need to talk to you about something."

April flashed a look at Gary's smiling face.

"What's up?" she asked, anxious.

Keith searched for the right words. "First, don't be upset but I told Gary everything."

Her jaw fell open. "What?"

"I'm sorry, Honey, but I had to. I was going crazy. Your argument was persuasive and logical and my position was based on insecurity, but I simply couldn't help it. I needed someone who knew me but wasn't you to listen and ask questions, so I made an executive decision and told Gary everything."

April looked at Gary, detecting a gleam in his eye she was sure Keith missed.

"Go on," she said.

"We've discussed it for the last two hours. Gary's tough. He asked hard questions and really made me take a look at myself. He's a good friend."

April tried to swallow but her throat was dry.

"I've decided you're right," Keith continued. "You're right and I'm in. All the way this time. Let's have fun with this. You can be as naughty as you want whenever you want. I trust you completely."

Irony twisted April's guts. About to admit everything, fate was handing her a complete pardon. Keith scooted closer and brushed a strand of hair off her face. He kissed her lips once, softly.

"Gary reminded me how utterly trustworthy you are. He encouraged me to be fearless. He said this was an amazing opportunity to create a life and a marriage unlike any other. I know you said similar things but they sounded so right coming from someone outside the relationship. Because he is an outsider to the situation his opinion is unbiased."

Keith took both April's hands. "Baby, you can fuck anyone you want."

April looked at Keith in disbelief. She glanced at Gary and saw manic excitement. Her confession died in her throat.

Or I can keep my mouth closed and get away with murder.

She hung her head.

"What's wrong, Honey? I thought you'd be thrilled."

"I am thrilled, my Love. Thrilled and humbled. I'm overwhelmed by your love. I feel unworthy of it."

Keith hugged her and her eyes went to Gary. He grinned and grinned.

What do I do? she wondered. *If I confess now Keith loses his wife and his best friend. He just trusted Gary with everything. My husband is so happy.*

A hard knock at the front door brought confused looks from all of them. Keith crossed the room and opened the door to a petite woman with brown hair wearing a baggy sweater over slacks. Her face was slightly familiar. He said hello.

"Save it. You may not remember me since we only met once. I'm Gary's fiancée, Helen."

She looked around Keith into the room. "All three together. How nice."

She waved at Gary. "Hi, Hun. Just wanted to let you know I'm aware of what you did and I'm breaking up with you." She threw a ring at him which hit his chest and fell to the floor.

She turned her gaze on April. "Fucking slut."

She faced Keith.

"You should know your wife has been cheating on you with my fiancé. Ex-fiancé. He bragged in an email to his friend, Todd, about banging that hot married chick April but then the dumbass left his email open. I found charge-card receipts. Club Diablo sound familiar? Sorry to tell you this way but knowing is better than not knowing."

She turned and walked to her car at the curb.

Keith stood stunned, clinging to doubt. Helen pulled away from the curb, burning rubber. He turned to face his wife and best friend. Their guilty faces erased all uncertainty. Their eyes dropped to the carpet. Hurt welled up inside Keith. His heart began a slow collapse, folding inward, tearing free from surrounding tissue like a black hole consuming itself.

"Why?" he croaked. He thought about demanding details but when, where, why, or how many times, seemed irrelevant. What mattered is that they had.

April crossed the room and tried to hug him but he shoved her away.

So many bits and pieces flooded his mind. So many clues he'd chosen to ignore.

"I gave you everything," he moaned. "Why would you do this?"

April tried again to hug her husband but he turned to Gary.

"Get out," he said. "Get out and never come back. Ever. You're a lying piece of shit. I trusted you completely. I'll never trust you again. How could I be so stupid?"

April tried a third time to embrace her man but Keith stepped past her to grab his car keys. Without another word, he headed for the garage. They heard his car start and Keith drive away.

Gary remained stoic but April started to cry. She told him to get out and stumbled to the bedroom. All around the little signs of their sweet marriage haunted her; knick-knacks and photographs from happy times. She'd ruined everything. She threw herself on their bed and wailed like a newborn. She heard the front door open and close. Now Gary was gone too and she was all alone. She covered her face with a pillow and cried.

***

April Willet returned the small blue weights to the rack and glanced around the advanced training center at the gym. She knew she belonged here. All around her others sweated and strained as they struggled to work themselves into shape. Trevor sat on the bench performing dumbbell military presses and Derek spotted him. She'd caught them gawking at her in the mirror several times.

Today she wore a light pink sports bra and the small raised bumps of her nipples lifted the fabric just slightly. Her gray booty shorts hugged her ass and she knew because she'd checked in the mirror at home that if she bent at the waist, she could flash a camel-toe that would raise the dead. She smiled.

Carla rounded the corner and aimed for the weights April was using.

"Can I grab those, Babe?"

"Sorry, I'm using them. You're welcome to work your sets in with mine."

"I'll come back."

Carla walked away to another machine. She watched the boys using the mirrors and when Trevor and Derek did not follow her with their eyes, she stopped to stretch her arms behind her back, thrusting her large breasts forward.

The boys stuck with April.

Carla tried several more times to draw the young men's attention but failed. April was working out and that's who they wanted to watch. After one final attempt, Carla exited the Advanced Training Center for the cardio machines.

April felt a rush of victory.

Eighty minutes later she completed her workout and headed for the parking lot and then home to shower. Trevor stood by her car. April admired the cool and casual way he held himself, trying to radiate confidence and masculinity.

"Hi, I'm Trevor. Can I talk with you for a minute?"

"Sure. What's up?"

"I've seen you working out and I wanted to introduce myself. I'm a personal trainer. You must have just joined this gym."

April laughed. "No, I've been coming here for months."

"Cool, cool. You think maybe we can grab a cup of coffee some time?"

April held up the back of her left hand, showing off her wedding ring. "Nope."

"I won't tell if you don't. What do you say? It's just coffee, right?"

She shook her head. "Nope."

His shoulders sagged. "Alright. Can't blame a guy for trying. You're a knock-out."

"That's sweet, Trevor, and it was nice meeting you. I'm sure I'll see you around."

They shook hands and April drove away.

No way will I fuck this up again.

Six months had passed since Helen dropped a bomb in their living room. April knew she and Keith had dodged divorce by the width of a hair. As it was, their marriage remained on unsteady ground. Luck smiled on her as months later Keith had stumbled across the Voodoo museum article on his own. He'd investigated thoroughly and four months after walking out on her, he'd picked up his cell and given her a call.

She'd been thrilled to see him calling. He had a million questions about the aphrodisiac effects. They talked awkwardly at first but gradually, with so much history together, they'd righted the boat and smoothed things out. Keith had moved back in four weeks ago.

Gary tried multiple times to apologize to Keith and explain what had happened, but Keith wouldn't hear him. April may have just the sliver of a reason but Gary had nothing. Keith never spoke to him again.

April confessed everything. She admitted the oil had certainly influenced her but she down-played the effect, trying hard to take accountability for what she'd done. Her choices had been her own. The aphrodisiac had not given her any ideas but made it easier to act on ideas she already had. Every betrayal had come from her own mind. She held nothing back. She dodged no responsibility. She took everything Keith threw at her without flinching. In time, his rage diminished as he shifted more and more of the blame onto the museum.

April resigned herself to the death of their adventures. She suspected Keith would never again want such an element in their marriage, so she was surprised when he brought it up. They'd finished dinner and sat watching a movie when Keith hit pause and turned to her.

"I miss it," he said.

April's heart jumped. She suspected what he meant but kept her mouth shut, fearful of jumping the gun and looking too eager. She waited.

"I cannot believe I'm saying this, given everything that happened, but if you subtract the shitty cheating stuff, we really had fun with it, didn't we?"

April nodded cautiously. "We did." She sensed he had more to say so she held her tongue. He was quiet for a long time.

"Everything goes through me first," he stated. "There will be no third chances."

She knew exactly what he meant and said she understood.

Now, as she drove home from the gym, she breathed a sigh, relieved she'd passed a test as big as Trevor. She wanted him, there was no denying it, and she'd rock his world so hard Carla would cease to exist, but she wanted Keith more, and Keith knew nothing about Trevor.

And that makes Trevor off-limits.

April turned the corner and saw the home she shared with Keith. Happiness filled her. They'd survived a catastrophe together, learned and grown from it, and now seemed poised for greater things.

I'm a lucky woman.

She pulled into the garage and shut the door.

Keith swirled April's clit softly, slipping his tongue down and into her hole. He licked all around her opening. He slipped his index finger in and gently rubbed her G-spot while returning his attention to her clit. When he had her moaning, he reached back and grabbed Michael by the cock.

I'll never get over how thick he is.

He tugged the man forward and Michael walked on his knees until his cock head almost touched her labia. Keith spread his wife open with his fingers and tugged Michael again. April jumped as the wide head made contact and Keith began to insert the bare-naked shaft. April had returned to birth control but Keith felt it was worth it to witness a hot stud fill his wife with cream. Keith loved watching April fuck, but he especially loved watching her fuck Michael.

He'd sent the man a text inviting him out to Las Vegas not long after his conversation with April. They both admitted there was no going back. They were hooked. The excitement of adding others to their bedroom was simply too much. Keith had considered his options and reached out to Michael.

This was the man's fourth trip to Vegas in the last six months.

Keith pushed April's thighs farther apart and pulled on Michael's cock. The head pushed in slowly at the same speed the air left April's lungs. Satisfied he'd gotten Michael started, Keith moved to his knees by her face and offered his penis to her mouth. April sucked him in. His wife looked amazing with a cock at each end and Keith began to think maybe it was time for a return to Diablo's.

I want to watch her take on three or four. I want to find that black guy that fucked her and watch a huge black cock split her open.

He pushed his penis against her tongue and she moaned. He began to fuck her mouth timing his strokes with Michael fucking her pussy.

"Hey Michael, maybe Victoria can give you some E for your next visit? We can all take it this time. April said she wanted to watch me suck your dick but there's no way I'm doing that without getting at least a little fucked-up first."

Michael laughed. "Right on. It would be hot to watch you both on my cock."

"Would you like that, April? Me and Michael high as fuck and banging you all night? I'd sure like that."

April moaned around the penis in her mouth. Her eyes were closed but Keith could see on her face she was right at home.

Visit my blog; MyEroticBunny.tumblr.com

Printed in Great Britain
by Amazon